F   1972   73442

Haning, Bob

Calamity at Apache Wells.

Willard Memorial Library
Willard, Ohio

Western

RULES

1. Books may be kept two weeks and may be renewed for the same period.
2. A fine of three cents a day will be charged on each book which is not returned according to the above rule. No book will be issued to any person incurring such a fine until it has been paid.
3. All injuries to books beyond reasonable wear and all losses shall be made good to the satisfaction of the Librarian.
4. Each borrower is held responsible for all books drawn on his card and for all fines accruing on the same.

*CALAMITY
AT
APACHE
WELLS*

by
Bob Haning

The scheme to rob the bank at Apache Wells had been carefully worked out. Kid Coxe was going to pick a fight with the sheriff and try to gun him down. And while the whole town was pounding down the street after the Kid, his partners in crime would break into the bank and be off before anyone could respond to the alarm. What they hadn't counted on was that the schoolmaster would know the Kid and be ready to give him an examination with some tough questions.

CALAMITY AT APACHE WELLS

CALAMITY AT APACHE WELLS

by

BOB HANING

LENOX HILL PRESS

1972

© Copyright 1972, by Lenox Hill Press

To

Arthur Hettich

Who has inspired me to greater things

Printed in the United States of America

1

The sheriff was a thick-set man with a wide face and a nose that was bent from being broken too many times, making it difficult for him to breathe. It was this inability to breathe during the August heat of Colorado that roused him from his bed in the room behind the office. He stamped his feet with the sullen, ill-tempered irritation of a man who is tired but cannot catch up on his sleep. He splashed water on his face from a battered washpan and blew violently through both nostrils in an effort to clear a passage. Bare to the waist, he stepped to the door and unconsciously began to rub his chest and arms as he studied the morning still of the town's main street in the lengthening dawn.

His eyes swept up and down the wide main street of Apache Wells, and the scene soothed at least a part of the frustration caused by his tiresome effort to breathe. He had made the peace in this town. And he had kept it peaceful.

He stepped down into the dust of the main street and moved from the boardwalk. Looking in one direction, his eyes settled on the livery stable; in the other direction the sloping hills rose to meet the sun, a red ball in a clear blue sky.

His town, Sheriff Clint Deane thought. It was beaten down now from the heat of the day before, and the day before that, and the weeks before that. It lay gasping in the dawn like a puncher exhausted from running down a wild steer calf, but he knew it would bounce back.

The Lucky-Seven Restaurant would open soon, and the men who owned the stores and the shops would be in talking to Vicky Deane, Clint's widowed sister-in-law, as they dug into their grits, eggs and bacon and swilled down mugs of coffee, lingering as long as possible to avoid starting the sweaty grind of a miserable day. The school bell would ring, and Master Shelby would be standing at the door, stern-faced, waiting for the strays to hurry to the schoolhouse. Douglas Vickers would drive in with his team of blooded stallions, open the bank and begin parceling out small loans. For this was a bad year, a very bad year.

His town, Clint Deane thought, would come alive soon, and he had better be ready. He moved out of the street to the steps, and for no reason at all that he could think of, because it was not like him to think of the past or reflect on it, he remembered the day three years before when he had rounded up a hole-in-the-wall gang that had tried to rob the Apache Wells Bank. He unconsciously reached down and rubbed the hard knot of a slug in his leg. There had been two other slugs, one in his chest and one in his shoulder, that the doc thought more important. By the time they remembered the leg slug, ten days later, he had told old Doc Marlowe, "Might as well leave it be, seein' as how I'm kinda gettin' used to it." And the slug had found a place in the thigh muscles and didn't bother him except when the weather was damp or the cold lasted several weeks.

He turned at the boardwalk just before stepping inside the office and looked across the street, lost in memory now. Before the hardware store a drunken cowboy once had resisted the attempts to be put in jail, where he could sleep off the effect of too much rotgut whiskey. Friends of the puncher had stepped in and nearly beaten Clint Deane to death with pistols; he had been in bed three weeks after that.

But there had not been many incidents like the fight with the hole-in-the-wall gang or the beating by the puncher's friends. There had been plenty of showdown fights and shootouts, but most of the time Clint Dean had not only used his fist-fighting ability and lightning draw, but also his brains. He relied as much on maneuvering against a man as he did on his fists or six-gun. The gun was always there, but he didn't use it unless it was necessary. There was something about odds. They had been explained to him one lazy afternoon by a poker dealer who later had died when a cold-eyed puncher drilled him neatly between the eyes for dealing from the bottom of the deck. He had used a new word in explaining why the raw-boned, hard young Clint Deane should not trust his life solely to his gun. "Statistics, Clint, will get you in the long run if you lean on your gun hand. The odds and weight of statistics will catch up with the best some day."

But the odds had not gotten Clint Deane yet. At twenty-eight he was known and he was respected, with a lot of fear in the respect. But more widespread than fear or respect was his reputation for being fair. There wasn't much more of a recommendation a man needed, especially if he had a bone-handled six-shooter that could come into play as fast as Deane's.

The sun was well above the eastern slopes when he stepped back inside the office and beyond to his room, where he began to shave. When he finished, he put on his last clean shirt, strapped the gun rig around his middle and headed for the Lucky-Seven Restaurant.

Vicky Deane, a slim, dark-haired woman under thirty, walked out of the kitchen with a platter of grits, eggs and butter for the young man sitting alone in the corner. He wasn't very tall, and he was frail. He sat quietly, and from the amount of dust on his clothes and the look of the black stallion at the rail, Vicky Deane sized him up as a drifter, or a puncher on the way back home. He wore a six-gun, tied down, but then a lot of men did that these days, copying the gunfighters; not, Vicky Deane knew, because they wanted to be gunfighters, but rather because the tie-down insured a fast draw under any circumstances. She put the platter of food before him and studied his face. He couldn't be more than twenty, and she was about to turn and forget him as just another rider when she saw his eyes.

He tried to smile. He showed even white teeth in the attempt to smile, but it did not change the expression that she saw in his eyes. She drew back, nearly stepping into a man's chair at the adjoining table. The boy's eyes were crystal-black and moist-looking, as if there might be frost on them.

"Somethin' wrong, ma'am?" he asked.

"No—I mean—I'm sorry." She smiled faintly.

The young man turned to his food and began eating hungrily.

Back in the kitchen, Vicky Deane peeked through the door. She was not given to that kind of schoolgirl behavior. She was a tough-minded woman who three years before had rented an empty store from the bank and opened a restaurant, this taking place shortly after her husband's death, and then out of necessity. She did it over the protests of the town fathers, who feared a woman alone in a restaurant would be a source of trouble from every drifter and trail hand who stopped to eat. "She's too danged pretty!" was the common complaint. And she was. But Vicky Deane had the sympathetic backing of the Apache Wells Bank, who, knowing the town needed a good eating place, had extended her credit.

Vicky Deane went right ahead with her plans, without resisting the town, and made her point with excellent food at fair prices, a clean dining room and quick service. The fact that she made the choicest apple pie and served the best coffee in Colorado helped not a little. And in the three years she had operated the Lucky-Seven with the Mexican cook, she had earned a reputation for taking care of herself. Not once had Clint Deane, her dead husband's brother, been called to settle any disturbance at Vicky's place. She did right well with a frying pan, and there was more than one puncher who had been flattened when he grabbed Vicky or tried to pinch the full breasts. All of this added up to experience and knowledge of the men she served. Some of them had been notorious gunmen whom Clint Deane had politely but firmly told to keep moving after they had finished Vicky Dean's pie and coffee. Some had

CALAMITY AT APACHE WELLS 13

been more difficult. Some of them had been rude, some of them polite, some of them talky and show-off, some of them quiet and within themselves. But all of them had been just what they were.

The boy sitting at the table was something else. There was a cold bloodless energy here that would never show sentiment or sympathy. Yet all he had done was order bacon and eggs and speak softly and politely to her when she staggered back after looking into his eyes.

She saw Clint Deane walk into the room, toss his hat to the rack and sit down with his back to the young man. Why didn't Clint notice him! Vicky Deane said to herself.

She filled a cup with coffee, burning her thumb in her haste, and pushed through the door. "Mornin', Sheriff." She said it loudly and glanced to see if the young man had heard her. He did not look up or give any indication that he had heard or, if he had, that he cared.

"Good mornin', Vicky," Clint said, surprise crossing his face at the greeting.

"Hot last night, wasn't it, Sheriff?"

"I couldn't sleep very much." Deane shook his head.

"Ah—how do you want your eggs, Sheriff?" She looked at the young man again, but he continued to eat.

"How do I want my eggs? Why, Vicky Deane, what's come over you? I've been eatin' a half-dozen eggs sunny side up with ham every mornin' fer the last three years." Clint grinned. "And what's this sheriff stuff? You mad or somethin'? You been callin' me Clint long 'fore you were ever hitched to my brother. Maybe you didn't get too much sleep, either."

II

While Clint Deane was waiting for his breakfast, while the frosty-eyed young stranger was quietly digging into his grits and eggs, while the sun was climbing in the Colorado sky, Austin Bailey was sitting before a coffee fire and studying the tracings on the ground. "This is the main street," he said to the four men around him, and pointed to a double line. "Here's the Apache Wells Bank on the corner, here's the Lucky-Seven Restaurant, the hardware store, the dry goods store, the feed and grain stalls, and then the Golden Nugget Saloon on the corner. There are other stores and houses on both sides of the street as you head in one direction toward the livery stable."

Austin Bailey pushed his hat back on his head. "Now Kid Coxe is already in town. He's gonna follow that hard-nosed lawman 'round till exactly eleven forty-five, which is when we will come into town from different ends. I'll go the northern way and start buying something at the hardware store. You, Grady, will go into the Lucky-Seven and have a cup of coffee and nothing else—jus' a cup of coffee."

The thick-necked man nodded.

Bailey continued, "Alex, you go in an' start talkin' horses to the feed store man. Todd, you go into the hardware store and buy some cartridges—might as well get a lot; we might have to do a little fightin'—"

Todd Bain broke in: "But you said there wasn't any possibility of there being a posse comin' after us."

"No, an' I don't think there will be. But we're goin' down into Comanche country, and you might have to do a little defendin' against 'em," Austin Bailey said patiently. If there was one characteristic that made Austin Bailey different from any of the other cruel range scavengers in Colorado, it was his slow, deliberate patience. In everything, Austin Bailey thought before he spoke or acted, except when he pulled his six-gun. Then his voice was muffled by the fanning blow of shots jerking into someone who had let the patience lull them into overconfidence. "Now, Curt, you'll jest hang 'round in front of the saloon an' keep your carbine handy. Kid Coxe is gonna pick a fight with the lawman an' gun him. Then when the whole town is tearin' off after the Kid on that streak-of-lightnin' horse of his, one by one we jest move in on the bank. Then we leave one by one when we're finished."

CALAMITY AT APACHE WELLS   17

"Where do we meet the Kid?" Alex Mayer asked.

"We don't meet him till we get to the other side of the border," Austin Bailey replied. He stood up. "Yo'all got it straight now? There's a helluva lot of cash in that Apache Wells Bank. These poor people have had a rough year down this way, and Douglas Vickers is a good old soul who will dole out to friends and the like. I figure he's got eighty, maybe ninety thousand in cash."

"Ain't but one thing I don't understand," Todd Bain said, pulling at his holster. "How do you know there ain't gonna be a posse?"

"Did you forget 'bout Coxe? What'n the hell you think is gonna happen when he pulls down on that lawman an' gets him? Every man an' child in Apache Wells is gonna pile out after him."

"An' if Coxe don't get the lawman?" Grady Potts asked.

"You ever seen anybody that was gonna beat the Kid to the draw?" Bailey asked.

"No. But damn it, that Clint Deane packs a heavy reputation," Curt Hawkins complained. "I didn't jus' hear the stories 'bout him an' Tad Blazer; I saw the fight. Dean downed Blazer 'fore he could clear leather."

"You know how old Clint Deane is?"

"He ain't got any gray hair," Bain said.

"No. But the Kid is still a boy, an' his hand is

like a bolt of lightnin'. There's eight, maybe ten years difference in ages an' jest plain gall. An' one more thing—the Kid is active. He's had gun play that forced him to be at his best, while Clint Deane has been sittin' 'round on his fat behind an' haulin' drunks to the pokey. No!" Bailey, a tall, ramrod-straight, sharp-eyed man, shook his head. "Not on your life! The Kid will down Deane without a hitch."

They might have been bulling, just range hands making coffee talk, stealing a little more time from the ramrod of the outfit before they hit the saddle for a long day's ride. They were no different from hundreds of others who worked for wages. They were like the men Vicky Deane served in the Lucky-Seven. In their eyes, there wasn't any of the deep, black mystery that Vicky Deane saw in Kid Coxe's. But they were killers, and they would shoot a man down in the back more readily than face him, or bushwhack him in the darkness with a bullet in the back of the head. It was like any other morning when range men gathered around the coffee fire and discussed their plans for the day; only instead of talking about herding strays or branding calves, hard, dangerous work in itself, they discussed holding up the Apache Wells Bank.

They had absolute confidence in Austin Bailey's nephew, Kid Coxe, and his fast draw.

When they kicked out the fire and moved toward

CALAMITY AT APACHE WELLS

their horses, they goosed each other and played practical jokes on the fat man in the group. The skinny one had the driest sense of humor, so he thought of most of the gags. But instead of laughing out like the others, he would crinkle his eyes and maybe give out with a little snicker. That was Todd Bain.

While they worked with their horses, examining the animals and saddling up, Alex Mayer started singing an old hymn. Austin Bailey, in a powerful rich bass, carried the chorus alone, while the others hummed harmony behind him. Five men who had, for one reason or for many good reasons, become men who lived beyond the law and would kill a man as soon as they would kill a rattlesnake. But when it came to everyday things, like coffee and horses and how to move a lazy herd or the best way to fix a lariat, they were not too different from the men who worked for their money and considered killing a cardinal sin.

When the sun was good and high, they moved down out of the timber and headed west to ride the twenty miles to Apache Wells. An hour later, several of them broke off and urged their broncs into a gallop to make a big wide loop around Apache Wells and approach the little town as though they were coming in from New Mexico.

"Fine mornin'," Todd Bain said to Austin Bailey, who rode with him.

"Yep. Fifth week of the drought, I heard a feller say a week ago in Shiprock. No clouds in sight, either. These poor people shore is takin' a beatin'."

"Still a nice day," Bain said.

"Yep."

They rode in silence, enjoying the morning and at the same time wondering if they would see the sun set that evening. Though neither of the men would admit it, each had felt a curious excitement since the Kid had left camp the night before. There had been something irrevocable in the way the Kid had slipped into the saddle and drifted off into the darkness with only the barest nod of his head. Bailey thought about the moment now. He could have stopped the Kid and in turn convinced the others to try something else in another part of the state. But Bailey saw himself standing beside the coffee fire watching the slim young man move into action, and would eventually bring them to the bank.

The riders let their ponies find footing to the top of a rise and rested a moment, staring down into the valley that stretched into nothingness. A dusty road wound through the center like a giant snake, and a cloud of dust rose in the distance.

"Ain't that the stage?" Bain asked.

"'Spect it is," Bailey answered.

"Might be Injuns," Bailey replied, studying the dust.

"But there ain't been no talk of Injun trouble 'round here."

Austin Bailey snorted and spit. "Injuns don't need talk before they hit. They jest hit, an' the talkin' is done afterwards."

They watched until they grew tired of the scene and allowed their broncs to move down into the flats for a solitary ride across the valley that led to Apache Wells.

III

O'Malley fired carefully, as carefully as he could considering the way the stage was bouncing. The Injuns seemed to be slackening their attack, but he wasn't sure. He squeezed the trigger and the carbine barked; then he grunted deep within himself as he saw the body of a half naked savage jerk crazily backward and slip from a racing pinto. He jacked another shell into the chamber, fired again and missed. The rifle was empty.

"Gimme 'nother rifle, quick!" he said over his shoulder to the man struggling against the pain of an arrow embedded in his shoulder.

"We're outa ammunition—" the man said with a gasp.

"Can't be!" O'Malley said. He turned from the side of the stage door and examined the gun-belt webbing, the boxes and the two six-guns. Not another load could be found.

O'Malley began to curse. He jerked himself up and

CALAMITY AT APACHE WELLS

stuck his head out of the window and yelled up to the driver. "Ammo!" he screamed. "Gimme your gun an' belt!"

The driver, a half-breed, uncommonly ugly and in his sixties, had dropped down into the boot and was driving the six-horse team with more skill than O'Malley could remember or thought possible. At breakneck speed, the driver that O'Malley called Big Foot had wound the stage through half the night while the Indians followed, spurred on by the reappearing brave that O'Malley identified as Spotted Pony.

The driver screamed as loudly as he could. "No gun—no gun—no bullets!"

O'Malley dropped back into the bottom of the stage. That did it. Everything depended on the driver now. As soon as the Indians saw that there wasn't any return fire coming from the stage, they would close in. O'Malley wouldn't be able to do a thing.

O'Malley, a relief driver, closed his eyes against the agony of his hands. He had forgotten about them in the furious defense. And he closed his eyes against the bloody face of the young woman sprawled on the seat opposite him. "Give her some water," he said to the little man.

"She's unconscious," the man replied weakly.

"Jus' as well," O'Malley replied.

He was a big man, nearly six feet five and thin

as a rail. He opened his eyes and stared at his hands. They were blackened, and the skin was sloughing off the palms. If he hadn't pulled out the tar-dipped, flaming arrows the Indians had fired into the body of the stage, they would have been burned alive or been slaughtered by the savages the moment they stopped and tried to escape.

O'Malley looked out of the window. The Indians were being careful. They were keeping back out of range, but they were still following, and there was no doubt in O'Malley's mind as to what they planned to do.

The stage lurched crazily, and there was a sickening interval when O'Malley thought the vehicle was going to turn on its side. But at the critical moment he heard a sharp report and knew that the driver had snapped his whip on the big lead stallion—the animal had jerked the stage straight.

He twisted his lanky body around and pushed his ear close to the face of the woman. "She's still breathin'," he said to the little man, "but it sounds like she's gurglin' in a bucket of water."

"Where did the arrow go in?"

"Just below her shoulder blade."

"It might have punctured a lung," the little man said. "That would account for the blood from her mouth an' nose."

O'Malley could hardly move his hands now. And

CALAMITY AT APACHE WELLS 25

they began to pain him as nothing had ever done before in his life. He crawled awkwardly back to the side of the door and stared out. The Indians were still there and moving in closer.

"How much more to Apache Wells?" the little man asked of O'Malley.

"Hour—maybe a little longer."

"Think we'll make it?"

"Mistuh, I don't know. I jus' don't know," O'Malley said, fighting hard against the vague feeling that was taking over in his mind. He shook himself to stay conscious.

"Do you think," the man said, "that you could give me a little water, Mistuh O'Malley?"

O'Malley turned around and tried to pick up the canteen that had been wedged underneath the seat. His fingers stiffened, and he could not move them. He looked up at the little man. "I can't, mistuh. I'm sorry. I jus' ain't got the strength."

"Of course. I'm sorry."

The Indians came in again. The horses, nearly exhausted from the terrible race, were slowing down as they approached the middle of a slight rise in the trail. O'Malley watched. Spotted Pony was well in the lead, waving his rifle and pressing forward. The others followed, their voices screaming out with seemingly inexhaustible power. "Here they come," O'Malley shouted. "They'll get us now."

But O'Malley was wrong. The driver of the stage had also timed his move with that of Spotted Pony's braves. He stood up in the boot and curled the big whip out over the heads of the horses again and again. They jerked at their harness. The stage lurched forward. The driver was screaming at the team, and the big whip was stinging the rumps of the horses and drawing blood through their hides. The animals broke in a frenzy. The stage rolled to the top of the rise a hundred yards ahead of the Indian braves. Once over the hill's crest, the driver really began to work his whip. The horses were wild with pain and trying to get away from the curling lash of the half-breed Indian driver's rawhide whip. The stage was nearly at the bottom of the rise, with good roads ahead, before the Indian party topped the rise in back of them. They pulled to a stop. Spotted Pony held up his hand. It was no use to press on. Their ponies were exhausted, and they were getting too close to the white settlement.

With ugly, determined hatred, Spotted Pony vowed to his braves that they would see the blood of white men run over the horses' hoofs before the sun went down that night. He saw the stage disappear into the cloud of dust rising behind the pounding hoofs and turned his pony around, riding back the way they had come to a place he knew where they would rest and he would plan.

CALAMITY AT APACHE WELLS

O'Malley saw the Indians stop on the rise, and though he knew it meant that they were safe from being butchered, one look at his hands, at the dying woman on the seat, at the little man, unconscious and face down on the cushions, and O'Malley was certain that he would never forget this day as long as he lived.

He slumped back. His hands hurt so badly he could hardly breathe. If he had shot a little higher, they might have avoided this. And the little man, who was so quiet and nice, and the pretty young woman wouldn't be near death. He'd always been a lousy shot. Why'n the hell couldn't he be a spitfire like that damned Clint Deane!

The tall gaunt-faced man leaned his head on his pulled-up knees and cried with rage against his inability to hold off fifty savages.

IV

Most of the others had gone by the time Master Shelby came into Vicky Deane's Lucky-Seven. School did not start until nine in the morning and lasted until four. There had been much discussion about the hours when he had come to Apache Wells three years before, a thick-necked, wide-shouldered man who wore a pearl-handled six-gun and did not look or sound like a schoolteacher. But the schoolteacher had explained that right away. "Young minds are not awake early in the morning. They play very hard during the day and try to burn up their energy. But they don't. They use most of it sleeping hard. Nine o'clock is when school starts."

And when the children of Apache Wells began to be lax in bringing in completed homework assignments, Shelby soon deduced that before they came to school they were working three and four hours at various chores. He had Douglas Vickers announce a special meeting and laid the law down cold and hard. "I'm the best goddamn schoolteacher west of Kansas City and will teach your young uns right. Now you got to make up your minds whether you want them taught right or not at all, because I ain't gonna have any half-assed students grow up into quarter-assed men and women. You do it my way, or I'll pack my books and move on."

That didn't sit so well with some of the folks of Apache Wells, especially hardware store owner Silas Grover and his brother, Ted, who ran the biggest saloon in Apache Wells. Both men—Silas had three boys and Ted had two boys and a girl—had worked their children before the school bell rang. They argued that, above the cost of maintaining the shed that served as a school, the cost of books, Shelby's wages and his house, they would have to hire extra men to do the work their children had been doing. "If they ain't worth the extra money, then keep 'em home," Shelby had replied stonily to the brothers.

And it was not too long before the good folks of Apache Wells knew they were buying a good thing. A seventeen-year-old boy had shown such brilliant understanding in law that he could quote page after page of law journals, take both sides of a case and argue either side to a winning conclusion. That he would run for the State Legislature when he became of age was a proud and openly discussed subject which increased community self-esteem. But perhaps

Shelby's most important, immediate victory came through a blue-eyed nine-year-old girl who had read and understood a tangled contract binding her father to a land deal that would have deprived the family of their spread. They ran the speculator out of town, stuffed the little girl with candy and cake, and then marched down to Shelby's and presented him with a quarter-keg of whiskey, which they knew the schoolteacher loved as dearly as he did his books.

Master Shelby and Clint Deane had regular run-ins over the loud and profane arguments Shelby would get into in the Golden Nugget Saloon on Saturday nights, but never once had the two men come to blows. There was mutual respect between them. But though Shelby slept in jail some Saturday nights, never once had anyone found him out of the schoolroom when he was supposed to be there, nor was he ever unshaven or untidy in his dress. He worked the children hard, but at the end of the term, when they held recitals on the meadow that served as a playground they knew their spelling, their arithmetic and their history—world, American, and what was more important, Colorado.

"Good morning, Master Shelby," Vicky said when the big schoolteacher came into the restaurant. "What's that you're reading?"

"Dickens has a wonderful imagination. He can tell a—" Shelby looked up. His eyes focused on the young man sitting in the corner, nursing a cup of coffee and watching them. The restaurant was absolutely still for a full five seconds as the men stared at each other.

"John Coxe!" Shelby said.

Vicky turned around. The young man smiled. "Howdy, Mistuh Shelby."

Shelby got up and walked over to the table and looked down at the narrow-shouldered youth. "What on earth are you doing in Colorado?"

"Driftin'," John "Kid" Coxe replied. He smoked, hunched over his coffee, leaning on his arms. His eyes softened just a little. "I didn't know you was teachin' in 'Pache Wells."

"How could you know?" Shelby sat down opposite him. "How is your mother?"

If the lad was uncomfortable, he did not show it. He continued to lean over his coffee and stare Shelby in the eye. Vicky tried to find some excuse to stay around. That someone should know this wild thing that had blown into her restaurant, especially the schoolteacher, was too unusual for her to absent herself. She began to fuss with the tables nearby.

"Both Maw and Paw cashed in some time ago," the boy said. Then, looking straight into Shelby's eyes, he added softly, "Suh."

"Is that why you left Lincoln?"

"No. I was run out. The sheriff told me to get

goin'. An' you know how Mistuh Dodge was. I got," Kid Coxe said. He dropped his cigarette in the remains of the coffee. He smiled suddenly at Shelby, who sat with his arms full of books. "Them things the young uns done in school? I know they mus' be. I recognize the way you made us make composition books, with that special sewin' 'long the seams."

"Did you go to work?" Shelby asked, putting the books to one side and nodding affirmatively in answer to the question about the composition books.

"Kinda," John Coxe said. "But I didn't work long, I punched steers fer a spell; then I jest drifted."

"Ever do any more reading about science?"

"Ain't but one science that'll do a man any good, Mistuh Shelby." Coxe's hand flashed to his side and returned with unbelievable speed, the six-gun leveled and cocked. It was the fastest move Shelby had ever seen. It was perfect, fluid motion. And he saw that the eyes were cool, without excitement, and the hands were as steady as a church organist's.

Kid Coxe put the gun away, and only then did the two men notice that Vicky Deane was standing as if struck dumb, looking at the six-gun.

"I'm sorry, ma'am," Kid Coxe apologized. "I didn't mean to scare you." He tipped his hat back at an angle. "I don't usually do that unless—" He stopped under the steady gaze of Shelby and Vicky Deane, suddenly looked down at his hands, and

CALAMITY AT APACHE WELLS   33

blushed like a schoolboy caught kissing a girl.

Vicky went into the kitchen without a word, her heart tight. You didn't often look into the eyes of a living extension of death. But that was the unmistakable frost she had seen earlier. Detachment. Indifference. Cold appraisal. She leaned against the sideboard and clutched her throat, suddenly unable to breathe.

"That was the most amazing thing I've ever seen," Shelby said quietly to Kid Coxe.

Coxe nodded, a short bob of his head. "I know it. I guess I'm the best man that ever lived." And he nodded his head again, as if affirming on re-examination an idea he'd stated too hastily. "Best man with a six-gun."

"What are you doing in Apache Wells?"

"Business." The chilly manner in which Coxe said it made Shelby back away. He picked up one of the composition books. He held it out to Coxe, who took it and opened it to the first page. He glanced up quietly, accusingly. "All of 'em science, or did you jest pick out this one in particular?"

"All science," Shelby said. "Maybe it's fate that I should come in here with the science compositions—which has never happened before in the years that I've been teaching."

Shelby watched the face as the lad read the first page. There was no hint of a change as the eyes skimmed over the writing. He turned a few pages, glanced through the book rapidly and handed it back to Shelby. "I left town 'cause I killed a man," he said suddenly. "It wasn't too long after you left. I went to live with an uncle up in Montana. I been 'round since then."

"Ever think about going on to medical school?" Shelby asked, and noticed that Vicky Deane was again messing with the tablecloths.

"No. That ain't no good any more. I'm too old. I ain't done nothin' but sleep with the open sky over my head since we was back in Lincoln, Mistuh Shelby." He turned to look out of the window at the slowly increasing morning activity in the main street of Apache Wells. "I animal-doctored a spell, but I didn't have no interest in horses or steers."

"No," Shelby said quietly. "It isn't the same."

Kid Coxe stood up and put on his hat. "I gotta take care of my horse, Mistuh Shelby. It's been nice seein' you again."

"Don't go, John. Sit and have another cup of coffee and let's talk."

"I ain't got no time fer your kind of talk any more, Mistuh Shelby. You might say it was kid's stuff, dreamin' 'bout being a doctor an' goin' to that school back East. I thought 'bout it once in a while, an' I had to laugh. Where'n the hell would I get the money to go to medical school? Ever think 'bout that,

CALAMITY AT APACHE WELLS

Mistuh Shelby?"

"That wasn't as big a problem as some others you had, John," Shelby said.

"I gotta be goin'." He hesitated and then offered his right hand, which Shelby saw was a distinct act of good faith and trust, since it was his gun hand. Shelby stood up and shook Coxe's hand firmly. "Luck to you, Mistuh Shelby."

He walked out of the door, a thin, quiet little figure that was all within himself, but was not tight. It was just that nature had made this young man aloof from things that other men would consider important.

Vicky Deane watched him leave. "He paid me ten dollars for breakfast," she said to Shelby. "Ten dollars!"

They both watched him as he approached the stallion at the hitching rail, and though Vicky did not see it, Shelby was not surprised when the slim rider glanced up and down the street without moving his head a bare inch in either direction.

"He was a student in my last school back in Lincoln, Nebraska. His mother was a prostitute and his father was a drunken mule skinner who beat him every night when he came home and found another man with his wife," Shelby said without emotion. "I've seen him take a pocket knife and dissect a live rattlesnake with one foot on its head—examining, looking, curious. He used to come to class with the brain of a field mouse floating around in clear corn liquor in a canning jar and watch and study it—"

Vicky Deane gasped.

Shelby looked up. "Not cruelty, Miss Vicky. Curiosity. I've never met another mind with the absolute detachment that John Coxe's had when he was eleven and twelve years old."

"What is he doing here in Apache Wells?"

Shelby did not answer right away. At that moment Douglas Vickers drove past the Lucky-Seven in his buckboard with the blooded stallions stepping high, necks arched and manes flouncing. "I don't know."

When Shelby looked out of the window, he saw that Kid Coxe did not turn around when Vickers stopped before the bank on the corner.

V

Deane knew his town too well not to notice there was something alien to the routine morning activity of Apache Wells. He took his solitary walk up and down the full length of the main street, speaking with Silas Grover, Douglas Vickers and Ted Grover, and saw Master Shelby head for the Lucky-Seven with an armload of children's books. He stopped near the saloon and watched Ted Grover sweep out. "You got anything on your mind, Ted?" he asked.

"Me?" Grover said around the stub of a cigar clamped between his teeth. "Naw—nothin', Clint."

Deane moved on down the street to the livery stable. He found the stable boy pitching hay and saw that his black had been grained. He patted the animal's neck and sucked absently on a blade of straw.

He walked back into the street, his intuition stronger than ever, alert for the thing that was out of whack. He saw nothing, heard nothing. The men from outlying spreads were drifting in now, some of them with buckboards, stopping before the hardware store or approaching the bank cautiously, because their pride was touched by having to ask for a loan. Some of them went into the Golden Nugget Saloon.

He patrolled the street, greeting those he knew, examining their faces, searching for something, anything that would put his mind at ease.

The thing that Deane felt was so strong that he had sweated through his shirt before he reached the church at the opposite end of town. He leaned against the log railing around the bubbling well and drank a cup of the hard, cold water, splashed some in his face and cast his eyes down the long street.

The sun was beginning to heat up, though it was only eight o'clock in the morning. It was going to be another hot day, with no rain in sight.

"Dammit!" Deane complained aloud. Maybe he was wrong. Maybe he was letting the heat get him, or the fact that he hadn't been able to sleep the night before. He certainly wasn't in a tolerant mood. He recognized his own uneven temper and tagged it correctly: boredom, excessive heat, lack of sleep, more boredom.

Nothing he did would negate the tension that was building with each tick of the clock. There were a few drifters in town, saddle bums who would hang

CALAMITY AT APACHE WELLS

around town a day or two, eating, drinking, then drifting on.

His eyes raked Kid Coxe when the youth came out of the Lucky-Seven. Every detail of Coxe's manner was considered; also the withdrawn, careful eyes, the dusty clothes, the careful outward angle of the gun rig nestled on his right hip, and the black stallion at the rail that looked as if it could probably fare well in any race. But there wasn't anything there; just another drifter. He was sure he saw the young man and the horse move down the dusty street toward the livery stable.

All right, Deane thought. I'll walk up and down again, just once more. And then, if nothing comes around, I'll just put it down as heat and boredom and go sit in the shade in front of the office.

He shoved off from the log railing, a little reluctant to leave the bubbling, gushing sound of the spring water, and stepped out into the sun.

He passed the Lucky-Seven and glanced over to see Master Shelby talking to Miss Vicky. That schoolteacher had better watch his step! Deane thought. If he thinks he's going to step on my toes with Vicky, he is going to need more than some of his smart talk to get shed of me. He whirled into the restaurant, sweaty, angry, full of tension. "Ain't you 'bout ready to go to school, teacher?" he demanded.

Shelby and Vicky Deane looked up, startled.

Shelby frowned. "What's the matter, Clint?" he asked.

"I asked you a question."

"I haven't answered it," Shelby said quietly. He closed the copy book. "Hot day, isn't it?"

"How come you got so much time to hang around the Lucky-Seven?" Deane asked testily.

"What is this?" Shelby said, his frown deepening. "What in the name of Satan's come over you?"

"It—it—" Deane glared at Vicky. "How come he sits 'round here? You don't let anybody else hang 'round unless they're eatin'!" It was so near to being a complaining whine, the whine of an angry, jealous suitor, that both Shelby and Vicky laughed out loud.

"What's so damn funny!"

They continued to laugh. Deane spun on his heel and slammed the door on his way out. He stalked down the boardwalk and rudely shoved past several men leaving the general store. "Get the hell outa the way!" he barked.

Deane walked a full block before he slowed his pace and allowed himself to think about Shelby and Vicky. What the devil was wrong with him! Every morning Master Shelby ate his breakfast in the Lucky-Seven and was the last one to do so, because he didn't start school until nine while everybody else started earlier. He stopped in the middle of his stride and removed his hat. He wiped the sweatband and shook

CALAMITY AT APACHE WELLS 41

his head, his eyes never leaving the street, taking everything in, missing nothing, searching.

He did not know how long he stood in the middle of the boardwalk, looking up and down the street; he was only jarred out of his thoughts by the ringing of the school bell. He would have to apologize to Vicky—and damn it, he would have to apologize to Shelby, too. He had to get a grip on himself. He shouldn't have flown off the handle like that and left himself wide open. Lucky there wasn't anyone else in the Lucky-Seven to see him act the fool. Neither Shelby nor Vicky, he felt sure, would mention his behavior to anyone. As if the town didn't already know that Vicky Deane was making up her mind about the two men. There had been an incident in Ted Grover's place when several loafers in Apache Wells had bet on who would eventually take the pretty lady up the steps of the church. She was certainly eligible, since her husband had been dead three years. The majority felt Vicky Deane would wed her dead husband's brother. Others disagreed.

He was about to turn and go back to his office when he heard the jangle of harness and the pounding of the stage and turned to see the team racing down the center of the street. The appearance of the stage told him immediately that it had been attacked by Indians. He breathed easier. He almost gasped with relief. Here, at last, was something.

The people of Apache Wells came out of their shops and stood on the boardwalk as the stage pulled to a stop before the doc's office.

Deane was the first in the dash to the stage. He jerked the door open, and O'Malley looked up and grinned. "H'lo, Mistuh Deane." And he passed out cold.

VI

Kathy Roberts had awakened earlier on that particular day and instantly thought of their trip into Apache Wells. She stood, dressed, and went to wake the oldest of her sisters. Together they went into the kitchen and began preparing breakfast for their father and Kathy's twin brother Paul, who had been up an hour already.

The fire in the kitchen stove was going strong when the others began to awaken, sleepy-eyed, yawning and hungry. Kathy was ready for them. She was always ready for them.

Her father stamped in, followed by her brother. The family sat down together and ate grits with pork fat poured on it as gravy and drank watered-down coffee. There was very little conversation. They knew, all of them, that their father was going into Apache Wells that day to take out a bank loan. They also knew that it had taken their father a long time to make this decision. Nothing else had been discussed in the house for weeks now.

Kathy had taken over the management of the house

when her mother died. She had, in a few short months taken over the position of sounding board for her father. This was not uncommon. But it tied Kathy to the house. There was little opportunity for her to go into Apache Wells and meet anyone.

Meeting someone was important to Kathy. Particularly Master Shelby.

When she was washing dishes with the three girls, the excitement of the trip to Apache Wells began to arouse the family.

"Gonna ask Mister Shelby about our makin' up the school we lost since Ma died, Kathy?"

"Hush, now."

"Well, are you?"

Her twin brother, Paul Roberts, moved out to hitch the team. Clay Roberts was shaving near the pump. He watched the crimson rise to his daughter's face. He spoke to the children sharply. "Don't pester Kathy now. You three girls get them dishes done and let Kathy get dressed fer town."

The children did as they were told. Clay Roberts looked lovingly at his daughter. Not once since his wife had died had the girl complained. "Daughter," he said, wiping his face and putting away his razor, "I'm gonna say somethin' you might not understand—" He hesitated. "I don't want to hurt your feelings none—" He paused again.

Kathy watched her father. Whatever it was, it was

CALAMITY AT APACHE WELLS   45

important. She sat down. She knew that her father liked to talk on his feet and that he also liked her to sit and listen. She had seen it all her life with her mother, and she had followed the pattern since becoming head of the house.

She waited.

Clay Roberts pulled on his shirt. "I never felt like it was necessary to have to talk to my girls with your mother 'round, but—" He paused again.

"What is it, Paw?"

His face reddened. "You like schoolteacher Shelby?"

"I do," she said.

"He said anything to you?"

"No."

Clay Roberts continued dressing. He walked out of the house without another word.

The wagon, driven by Paul Roberts, pulled out of the yard. The girls and boys were clustered around. They waved and shouted and followed the wagon to the fence, but neither Clay Roberts nor his twin son and daughter missed the hopefulness in their eyes. They did not ask for anything. They just hoped.

Paul primed the team with a hard lick from his whip, and the wagon began working its way into the trail. He brought the subject up again. He always had been able to talk to his sister. He grinned. Showing a foolish face, he nudged Kathy with his shoulder. "Seems to me that Master Shelby might have a little more on his hands these days than he can rightly handle."

Clay Roberts picked it up. Perhaps he could say what he wanted to say as a joke. It had to be said. "Paul," he said, "ain't likely that schoolteacher Shelby will ever get hisself a horse to come out fer Sunday dinner, is it?"

"Not if he ain't ever invited."

"You think I oughta go and invite him?"

"What fer?"

Kathy looked quickly at her father. He turned his head away and slung a leg over the brake handle. "Why, to get them young uns into line, that's what fer."

"They out of line, Paw?"

"Can't you tell! Why, Paul, if we don't get that schoolteacher out to the house—some way or other—or get another set of horses to drive the young uns into school, why, we're gonna have a family of derned idiots."

"Sounds serious," Paul said, deadpan.

Kathy Roberts sat between the two men, holding her face expressionless against the smile that wanted to break out. "If you will get the books, I'll be able to teach them a thing or two."

"Won't do," Clay Roberts said. "Won't do at all. Them young uns have got to have serious teachin'.

CALAMITY AT APACHE WELLS   47

How can you do things in the house an' teach young uns at the same time?" He had to keep from looking at his son Paul, or they would both have burst into laughter.

Kathy said nothing. She thought about it, though. He—and she had lately begun to think of Master Shelby as he—might not come. Hadn't she heard the talk about him and Miss Vicky?

He was not the only man in town. Yet she was not unaware that Master Shelby was fast becoming the only one for her.

The wagon group settled into silence as they drew near Apache Wells. They did not forget about Master Shelby, or that their Kathy was isolated and would continue to be, doing her job taking care of the Roberts family, but they let this thought slip to another corner of their minds.

They thought about other things now.

They thought about the bank loan and what it would mean to them if they got it.

And what it would mean if they didn't.

Paul Roberts snapped his whip, and the team pulled into the main trail that would take them into Apache Wells.

Douglas Vickers was standing at the window watching the scene around the stage, noting the scars in the body of the carriage where the arrows had dug into the wood. When they had emptied the inside, they had left the doors open, and he could see the floor that was covered with spent ammunition casings. It had been a hell of a fight, he thought. It must have been a humdinger of a fight.

But he was not taken in emotionally by the incident. It was, after all, only one raid by an Indian party, and only four people had been touched by it. And from the word of his teller who had come back with the story, all of them would live.

From Douglas Vickers' point of view, the Indian attack was reduced to a simple problem. The owners of the stage line would have to replace the stage. They would first go to the Shiprock bank for a loan, and Vickers knew that old man Partride was in as bad a way as himself, and then the owners would come over to him. It would take about a thousand dollars, Vickers thought, to replace the stage, or get this one overhauled, fix up the insides and get a fresh set of lead horses. Even from his window across the street, he could see the split hoofs of the horses where they had been forced to run over rough ground and then to run on damaged hoofs.

"There's a young woman," the teller said in his ear, "name of Traynor. Poor thing, she took an arrow in the back, and the doc thinks she's goin' to have a hell of a time gettin' it out."

"Who is the man?" Vickers asked.

CALAMITY AT APACHE WELLS 49

"Tod McKinney—been down visitin' somebody in New Mexico. Come from up North."

"I've heard of a Tod McKinney in Cheyenne. Businessman. Wonder if it's the same man."

"I don't know, Mistuh Vickers." The teller turned at a cough in back of them and patted the bank owner on the shoulder. "Mistuh Vickers, suh, Mistuh Roberts is still waitin'."

"Oh, yes." Vickers turned wearily away from the window. "Roberts."

He sat down heavily at his desk. He had nothing to say to the man. Two hundred acres to the southwest, all of it grazing land, parched, burnt, bonedry, and his cattle dying like flies. The man wanted money on his spread to carry him over. Clayton Roberts, eight children, a widower. The man needed four thousand dollars, was asking for three, and Vickers couldn't give him more than five hundred. He hated himself. He hated this country. He hated Clay Roberts and men like him who had to come in with their sad, long, tight faces, with their pride tucked in their hats under their arms, and make their mark on the mortgage.

"Mister Roberts, you say you have seventy-five head on your land now?"

"Yessuh. But I got to be honest with you an' say that I ain't expectin' to find that many when I get back."

Vickers turned away from the straight answer. That was the trouble, damn it! If only they weren't so honest. If they were just a little sullen, or showed a little temper, it would be easier for him to put them off.

"Clay," he said heavily, "I know your place, and I know it's worth at least five thousand, but I can't let you have but five hundred."

"Five hundred?" Clay Roberts swallowed. "I got them young uns, Mistuh Vickers—"

Vickers slammed his fist on the desk. "Damn it! I know you got to feed your kids—"

"Yessuh," Roberts said, and looked over the tip of Vickers' head.

"There's so many others, Clay, just like you. I got to spread it around."

"I reckon you have, suh. But—" Roberts stood up, his eyes hard and unseeing. "I'll jest never mind 'bout the loan, then, Mistuh Vickers. Thank you jest the same."

"Sit down!" Vickers commanded, his voice sharp. "I'll give you seven hundred and fifty. And that's all I can do, the very last thing I can do."

Roberts sat down. Vickers shook his head. "Come in next week for the papers. I'll have them ready then. Take this over to the pay window and let the teller open an account." He handed over a bank draft. "For God's sake don't let those cattle go,

Clay. Even if you have to feed 'em at your own table, keep them alive until next year."

"I'll do it, if I have to drive 'em to Wyomin' fer winter grass," Roberts said.

"You may have to," Vickers said. He had to get out of there and have a drink. He had to get away from them for a few minutes. He took his hat and stomped out of the bank without a word to any of the others who waited patiently on the hard chairs outside the railing.

VII

Kid Coxe had finished rubbing down the stallion and personally haying and graining the animal, careful about its water, working around the stall with a minimum of movement and in a direct, purposeful manner. When he heard the noise of the arriving stage, he stepped to the door and looked down the street, wondering if Austin Bailey or maybe that hot-headed Grady had jumped it. It would be hell for breakfast if they had. He showed no emotion when he saw them taking the young woman out of the stage with her face all bloody, saw the neat man with the stub of a shaft still sticking through his black frock coat. And he narrowed his gaze when he saw the tall puncher's burned hands.

He finished with the stallion, saddled it, and took careful pains with the double cinch so that it would not be too tight and pinch his mount. When he was

CALAMITY AT APACHE WELLS 53

finished, he washed some of the dirt off in the watering trough out back of the livery stable, stripping down to the waist and exposing to the sun his whip-thin, narrow-boned body that was burned brown. When he took his shirt off, he looked very much like a young Indian.

He had digested the incident of the stage and concluded that it gave them a definite advantage. I might not have to waylay the big sheriff, he thought, if they are mad enough to go out after the Injuns. But even if they don't, they will be excited by the stage raid and not looking out for a raid against the bank.

Washed as clean as he could get without an all-over bath, the young rider shoved his hat to the back of his head and moved out into the sunlight toward the knot of men around the front of the doc's office. He stood on the outer edges, smoking, listening to their comments, an idle interest in his eye.

O'Malley came out first, his hands swathed in white bandages that already showed the thick gobs of grease with which the doc had covered his hands. "Somebody's gonna have to pour a few bottles of Ted Grover's rotgut whiskey down my gullet so I kin sleep," the big driver said.

"Does it hurt, O'Malley?" someone asked.

"Like they was still on fire."

Several men moved off toward the saloon with the

tall driver, leaving the door around the office free. Kid Coxe moved over a little to look inside, and his forehead wrinkled. The man was on the floor, and the woman was stripped down to the waist, her back and the ugly red gash of her wound exposed. The doc was working quickly, while the big sheriff and a half-breed Injun were holding her down.

Coxe watched while the doc made a long incision along the line of the gash and peeled back the layers of skin. The Injun turned away and then vomited on the floor, but he held onto the woman's wrist. The man in the frock coat began to moan.

"Hurry up, Doc; looks like your other customer is gonna need you pretty damn quick," Deane said.

"I got to get this arrowhead out!" the doc said. "It's pressin' against the lung, an' it might have gouged a hole in it, from the way she's bubbled up her nose and mouth with blood."

Kid Coxe looked at the man in the frock coat and then, before he knew what he was doing, he was inside the office. "I kin take care of this one," he said quietly to the doctor.

"Don't touch him!" the doctor exclaimed. "You go pokin' 'round after that stump, an' you'll tear him to pieces inside. He'll last." All the time the doctor was working feverishly over the back of the woman.

"Penetration ain't very deep. It's in the scapula,"

CALAMITY AT APACHE WELLS

Kid Coxe said, "and I think it's shattered the lower quadrant. Won't even be necessary to incise the wound to find out the damage done inside. You could practically see it, an' what you couldn't see you could feel out a little bit with your finger."

The doctor never stopped his work on the woman. "You had medical training?"

"No. Just read a little bit."

"Git to it, then."

Kid Coxe worked easily and surely. He took his knife and slit the cloth around the stubby shaft, examined carefully the angle of its penetration and tested it carefully. While the doc continued to work down through the layers of muscle, he glanced at Kid Coxe kneeling beside Tod McKinney and watched the hands that were not unlike a woman's, but were strong and steady, probe the angle and the set of the arrowhead.

"Well, get going," Deane said, watching the young man staring at the end of the shaft. "Whatcha waitin' for?"

Coxe did not bother to look up or answer. His attention and his thoughts were focused on the wound. He tested it again, and then with a firm, gentle pressure began to pull the shaft out. McKinney groaned, but Coxe continued the steady pressure. The shaft end moved a little and then stuck. "Uh-huh," Coxe said to himself. He looked up at the doctor. "Need a thing to separate the openin' a little."

"Over there." The doctor motioned to a black bag. Coxe crawled the few feet, rummaged around in the bag and pulled out a pair of pliers used for pulling teeth. "This'll do it," he said aloud.

While Deane watched, and with an occasional glance from the doc, Coxe inserted the closed snout of the pliers, spread them gently against the flesh and pulled again at the stub of the Apache arrow. The two-inch stub and the head of the arrow slipped out easily.

Still holding the wound open with the pliers, Coxe inserted his forefinger and briefly touched around inside. He looked up at the doctor. "Two pieces, about a half-inch each: you think they'll rest easy?"

"Can you get 'em out?"

"Sure."

"Get 'em out," the doctor ordered.

Coxe worked his finger in the open wound and pulled out one and then another small chip of bone. "How you gonna dress this thing?"

"Make it bleed and bind it in its own blood," the doctor replied.

Coxe hesitated. "How 'bout jus' burnin' it out? He's lost a lot of blood already. If we don't close up the wound an' let it bleed, it'll make him weak an' take him a longer time to get back on his feet. If you burn it out, you clean it, an' you give him

CALAMITY AT APACHE WELLS

a better chance of gettin' well faster."

"All right," the doctor said, and turned to one of the men who had gathered at the door again. "Get the fire poker and get it red-hot!" he ordered.

Coxe got up, stood beside the table and looked at the woman's back. "If the lung's punctured, how you gonna fix it?" he asked.

"You got any ideas?" the doctor asked.

At that moment he was down to the arrowhead. It was just deep enought to have ruptured the lung. "If you pull that thing out an' it's torn open the lung, she'll drown in her own blood," Coxe said.

"Damn it, I know it!" the doctor replied.

"An' I ask you if you've got any ideas?"

"If you don't do something fast, she's gonna die right here," Coxe said quietly. Throughout the operation on McKinney and his study of the woman's back, Coxe moved with the same light, effortless, unruffled manner he had exhibited when caring for his horse.

"I'm gonna pull it out," the doctor said, clenching his teeth.

Coxe's eyes hardened. Clint Deane saw the change in his face as he moved closer to see. But had he moved? It just looked as if he had moved in closer. The doctor pulled the shaft, and the blood spurted six inches, flowing over his hand.

"She's gonna die," the doctor said, and pressed his finger into the wound. "Damned Apaches!"

The blood had stopped momentarily, but all of them, even the half-breed Injun knew, that when the doctor took his finger out, Miss Traynor would die.

Coxe picked up the woman's wrist and felt her pulse. "She ain't got long," he said.

The doctor looked at Clint Deane and the half-breed and the men crowded in the doorway. "She's gonna die—"

Coxe had already decided there wasn't anything anyone could do for Miss Traynor and was now concentrating on the pulse. He wanted to know, but he was not conscious of wanting to know, every change that took place as the life ebbed out of the young woman's body.

"She's dead," he announced.

The doctor looked at Clint Deane and then at Kid Coxe. "Dead?"

He removed his finger from the wound, half expecting to see a spurt of blood cover his hand again, but the blood did not spurt.

The roar of a man outside turned their attention to the door, and the white-hot poker was brought in. Coxe turned from the body of Miss Traynor and dropped to his knees. He took the poker and cauterized the wound. McKinney's body quivered, and the man moaned. Coxe then handed the poker back to the nearest man, swabbed the freshly burned wound with a handful of grease and, after stripping the

CALAMITY AT APACHE WELLS 59

clothes off McKinney, bound the wound neatly and tightly.

The doctor sat in a chair and stared at the dead Miss Traynor, his hands still covered with the young woman's blood. "Those damned Apaches—" he said with no spirit in his voice at all.

Kid Coxe frowned slightly when Clint Deane covered the body of Miss Traynor with a sheet. He turned to Doctor Marlowe. "You killed her," he said quietly.

Deane and the others stared at Kid Coxe incredulously. The doctor moved his head slightly. "I know it," he said tonelessly.

"What'n the hell is this?" Deane demanded. "You got a helluva lot of nerve, stranger, tellin' the doc he killed her. It was an Apache arrow that did the job."

"No, it wasn't," Coxe said, wiping off his hands and staring coolly into Clint Deane's face. "He admits it. Ask him."

The doctor only nodded his head.

"How did he kill her?"

"That arrow didn't do more than jest barely bother the lung, but he cut the aorta when he pulled it out so fast."

"The what?"

"The biggest artery in yore body."

"Is that true, Marlowe?" Deane asked.

Coxe did not hear the answer. He was walking out of the office and pushing through the men who stared at him with disbelief in their eyes. He walked slowly down the boardwalk, a slight little man, hat on the back of his head, the picture of youthful indolence.

VIII

Following Kid Coxe out of the office, Clint Deane watched the figure of the strange youth and bit his lip. If what Coxe had said was the truth, what was he supposed to do about the doctor? He glanced back at the old man still sitting in the same position, his head sagging now, the blood of the woman still covering his hands.

"What you want to do with the man, Sheriff?" someone asked him.

"Take him over to the hotel, an' then see if you can't round up one of the ladies in town to take care of him. Where'd O'Malley go?"

"Over to Ted Grover's Golden Nugget to get drunk. Said his hands was hurtin' him so bad he couldn't stand it."

"Better stay with him, one of you men. I seen his hands when Doc cut the dead skin away, an' they were burned right down to the bone."

"I'll stay with O'Malley," the half-breed said behind Deane.

62 CALAMITY AT APACHE WELLS

Deane turned and looked at the body of Miss Traynor. "We'd better get Elder McIntyre to make a coffin for the lady. We'll bury her in the churchyard soon as everything's set."

The men nodded, and several of them went off to carry out Deane's orders. He continued to watch the slim figure of Coxe, wondering who the man was and what he was doing in Apache Wells. He himself had noticed how excited the doctor had been when the stage had arrived, and knew that if it hadn't been for the kid, the man with the arrow in his back might have died—even before the doc got to him. He turned back into the office suddenly and shook Marlowe by the shoulders. "Were you drunk?" he demanded.

Doc Marlowe had been nearing sixty when he had hit Apache Wells eight years before, a little before Deane himself had shown up. He did not have to tell Deane that he had been dead drunk when the shouts at his door had followed the arrival of the stage. The red lines in the doc's eyes, and on a closer look, the puffy sacks beneath the eyes and the bearded face spoke for the man. Deane turned away. What the hell! Even if he was a doctor, he had a right to get drunk once in a while.

He left the doctor's office and walked down the boardwalk, not seeing the young stranger any more, and headed for his own office.

CALAMITY AT APACHE WELLS

Doctor Marlowe sat very still, staring at the blood on his hands. *If I could only tell myself I didn't care*, he thought. *There have been hundreds that died at my hands, some of them due to mistakes just as bad as this. But it was always my secret. Now they won't trust me any more. I know they won't.*

He got up and began washing his hands, watching while the men fashioned a makeshift stretcher for the wounded man and carried him out of the office over to the hotel. *It won't take long before they'll stop calling me. And it's too late to start some place else.*

When he was alone, Doctor Marlowe wiped his hands and closed the door, then pulled back the sheet covering the body of the woman. The body was already stiffening. He had better set the neck and head straight, or it would be crooked in the coffin. He examined the wound. Yes, there it was, the aorta severed as cleanly as if he had done it with a knife. The dead flesh in his fingers, the old doctor in the heart of a wilderness thought back to the day in medical school when he had opened his first dead body and had held just such an artery as this.

Clint Deane sat with his heels propped on his desk and studied the toes of his boots. Some of the ache in his back from the unaccustomed tension of being around operations on human bodies was gone.

64 CALAMITY AT APACHE WELLS

He hurled his hat to the corner viciously and wiped the sweat from his eyes. Someone had dropped the mail brought in by the stage on his desk. He picked up the envelopes and began opening them, more in a vain hope that something would show up to take his mind off the scene in Doc Marlowe's office than from any official interest or personal curiosity.

There were the usual circulars: faces of men with cruel mouths and hard eyes that were wanted for murder, robbery, and a half-dozen different crimes. He studied them with unseeing eyes, sifting through them with only the most casual interest and study. A few names he recognized. Austin Bailey and Todd Bain, who had teamed up a long time ago. Their faces were like the others, the faces of men who might be dirt farmers or small cattlemen with a few head of tough, mangy steers, trying to scratch out a living from the Colorado soil.

There was one description without a picture in the same envelope with Austin Bailey and Todd Bain. "John (Kid) Coxe," it said, and the description was that of the youth who had saved the man's life in Doc Marlowe's office.

Deane sat up. It could be the same person. The circular said plainly that the man was quiet, young, slim, and rode a black stallion. But there were a lot of black stallions and a like number of men who were small and quiet.

Deane got up. The images from the operation, so heavy and sharp in his mind a few minutes before, had not blotted out completely the figure and manner of Kid Coxe. The thing that did it for Deane, the information that made him sure, was the one-line note on the bottom of the circular: "Known to have interest in medicine."

He folded the circulars of Austin Bailey, Todd Bain and Kid Coxe and shoved them in his pocket. He retrieved his hat from the corner where he had hurled it, straightened it out, checked his gun and stepped out of the office. The day had been wrong from the beginning.

He stood before his office and surveyed his town. He saw the slow unhurried movements, the deliberate ways that he knew as well and as surely as he knew the delicate trigger mechanism in his six-gun. Nothing had changed in the street.

Mrs. Grover was hurrying out of the alleyway in back of her husband's saloon and heading for the hotel. He grunted, appreciative of the meddling that always seemed to come with their goodness. They loved to take over.

His eyes swung around. Vickers waved to him from the bank window.

Deane waved back. His gaze moved on. Nothing wrong—yet. Nothing to get aroused over—yet. Except Kid Coxe. That might be something.

The day had been wrong, very wrong, dead wrong, from the beginning. He stepped off the boardwalk. He decided he would try the saloon first. A gunslinger had little chance to quench his thirst, they were on the dodge so much. It was entirely possible Kid Coxe would be in the saloon. But something in Deane's lawman instinct told him he was wrong. He could not explain it. He had stopped trying to explain his "hunches" a long time before.

He blew his nose. There was no relief. He tried again. He shook his head and pushed the worry out of his mind, wondering fleetingly if there was any use taking Doc Marlowe up on that talk about a hospital in San Francisco that might be able to help him. It would surely help to be able to breathe again.

He moved down the street slowly, very slowly. It was, Deane thought, a sign of a laughing providence that such a man should carry such a burden. Here he was, and he knew that he was—a hard-boiled lawman in a town that was his life—and he could not breathe properly.

He glanced at a clock through the bank window. Quarter to eleven. Where had the morning gone?

IX

Grady Potts, Alex Mayer and Curt Hawkins had ridden well to the south and were only a few miles outside of Apache Wells when they pulled up to a stop beneath the protective shade of a cottonwood tree.

"All right, Grady. You go on in, and we'll follow you about a mile apart," Alex Mayer said. "You got everything straight now?"

"Don't you worry none 'bout me. I'm jest hopin' that Coxe has already downed that lawman," Potts replied. He laughed good-naturedly, the way fat men will when they are about to do something they enjoy, waved over the top of his pony's head to Mayer and Hawkins, and galloped out of the shade toward the well-rutted road to Apache Wells.

Mayer and Hawkins slipped from their saddles and stood on the ground. When Grady Potts had disappeared around a small bend, Mayer turned to Hawkins and nodded. "Okay, you next."

Hawkins was a quiet man who rarely spoke. He moved with his bronc down to the trail, riding better than any of them except perhaps Kid Coxe, who rode better than any man Alex Mayer had ever seen; he did not bother to turn around and wave at Mayer, who watched him from the shade of the tree. In a few minutes, after he had rolled and smoked a cigarette, Mayer climbed into the saddle and sat his bronc in the shade while checking his guns, both carbine and six-gun. Satisfied, he urged the animal to step out into the sun and followed the other two into the trail that would lead to Apache Wells.

Austin Bailey and Todd Bain, on the other side of Apache Wells, decided they would ride in together. They had not forgotten the stage and its pounding drive across the flats, and though neither of them mentioned it in their solitary ride across the range that lay to the north of Apache Wells, they both thought about it and agreed it would be better if they went in together. There was a chance of better odds if they rode together, just in case something had gone wrong with the arrival of the hell-bound stage.

"You reckon Kid Coxe has already taken care of Deane?" Todd Bain asked.

"Don't see no reason why not," Austin Bailey said. "An' I'll tell you somethin' straight, Todd, though I wouldn't want you to ever mention it to a

CALAMITY AT APACHE WELLS 69

soul. I wouldn't much care if they'd downed each other by the time we get there."

Todd Bain looked toward his partner carefully. "Meanin'?"

"That Kid spooks me. It's his eyes, an' the way he'll jest gun down a man, with that six-shooter of his'n blazin' like forty, an' then walk away without a bat of an eyelash."

"I ain't never seen you shed no tears," Bain said.

"No, that's so. But I never got too much pleasure out of shootin' a man down, unless he had somethin' I wanted."

"I know. And I would sure like to get shed of that Kid, too. He spooks me, and that ain't no lie."

"We could fix that easy enough. We're supposed to meet him an' Alex an' Grady an' Curt south of the border, ain't we?"

"Yeah," Bain agreed slowly, turning to look at the man with the cruel, sly streak in him.

"Well, we didn't say which border. Seems to me the country is plumb filled with borders, jest naturally filled with 'em. We could take our pick, say one up Montana way."

"But you're actin' like the Kid has already been downed."

At that moment, Todd Bain pulled his six-gun and fired quickly into the brush twenty feet off. Bailey jerked around in time to see a rattlesnake writhe, headless, and then disappear in a wriggling ball into the brush. "That nephew of yourn is jest like that rattler," Todd Bain said. "An' jest as dangerous."

"Okay—but I ain't gonna do it. Somehow, shootin' kinfolk is somethin' I jest can't do."

"I'll do it," Bain said. "I would have done it long 'fore this if I hadn't worried 'bout what you'd do."

"Ain't no love lost 'tween us. He's jest a runny-nosed kid that was dumped on me when his paw an' maw kicked off."

"Then it's settled?" Bain said, blowing on the barrel of his six-gun and carefully replacing the cartridge.

"Any time you want to do it—that is, if Deane ain't put him down—"

"Deane ain't about to put him down. Ain't no man alive kin do that. It's like them stories you hear 'bout the Apache Indians and their double-hung bows. I don't think even Kid Coxe could get his gun out faster than one of them savage devils could string an arrow."

Bailey nodded his head. "I heard 'bout that. I heard 'bout how some of the Injuns could do that with a double-hung bow."

"I'll shoot that nephew of yourn in the back of the head. I'd never stand a chance facin' him," Todd

CALAMITY AT APACHE WELLS 71

Bain said, and Bailey turned to see if the man was smiling. But he wasn't.

They began checking their guns when they were a mile or two north of Apache Wells and the sun was high over their heads.

"Now you just rest easy, sir," Mrs. Grover said with husky sympathy as she patted the pillow for Tod McKinney. "Nothing to fret about now. Them bad old Indians are going straight to a lake of fire and brimstone for their acts of wilful destruction. They are nothing but savages, it is true, but the Good Book says you have to be born again to enter the kingdom of heaven, and if they don't get their naked unwashed bodies into a good Christian missionary station and meet their savior on bended knees, all their medicines and little sacks full of gewgaws and colored beads they think will save them will burn right with them in that place where Satan lives. Just you wait and see, suh. They will meet their maker on Judgment Day, and then you will see their heathen faces turn away with fear when the great judge tells them they have been living a no-account life, going around killin' good folks and murderin' blessed little children."

Mrs. Grover moved to adjust the cover on the bed. There was a strange stillness about the figure. She hesitated and then put out one hand to touch the

72 CALAMITY AT APACHE WELLS

flesh of the man. She gasped and stepped back. There was no question—the man was dead.

Deane did not find Kid Coxe in the saloon, or in the barbershop, or down at the livery stable. He stopped again in the Lucky-Seven Restaurant, where Vicky was preparing the tables for dinner. "You seen that young stranger that was in here this mornin', Vicky? The one that you wanted me to see so badly you nearly shouted out that I was the sheriff?"

Vicky Deane stopped her table cleaning and turned to stare at Clint Deane with her mouth open. "How did you know about him?"

Clint Deane showed her the circular. "He saved the life of one of the passengers when old Doc Marlowe was so drunk he did somethin' wrong to the woman's insides and she bled to death."

"I haven't see him, Clint," she said.

"You might. He may be by here to eat dinner. Don't say anythin' if you see him, but send me word."

"Clint—"

"Yes, Vicky?"

"What has he done?"

"Killer. Circular says he gunned 'bout a dozen men."

"Couldn't they have been fair fights?"

CALAMITY AT APACHE WELLS

"I don't want him for murder. He's also a bank robber," Clint Deane said. At the door, he turned back. "I apologize 'bout bustin' in here this mornin' an' behavin' the way I did."

Vicky tried to smile. "That's all right, Clint. But I think you had better apologize to Master Shelby, too. He likes you."

"That's the trouble. I like him, too. But I like you better." He stepped out of the door and walked away, leaving Vicky Deane alone with her thoughts about Clint Deane and Master Shelby, and the youthful, strange John Coxe, who had gunned a dozen men and was wanted for bank robbery.

He had to be in town some place, Deane thought. But where? He moved back down toward the spring, where several cattlemen were talking. He was reluctant to go into their midst. He knew they would either be talking about what had happened at Doc Marlowe's earlier or about the heat and the bad year, and he didn't want to hear any more on either subject.

He turned the other way, back toward the center of town, his walk slow, purposeful, his eyes scanning the town looking for the youthful and deadly John "Kid" Coxe.

He saw the half-breed Indian driver half carrying O'Malley out of the saloon and grunted with satisfaction that the man had managed to get enough liquor inside him to ward off the pain. Deane had seen a lot of burns in his day, but nothing like O'Malley's hands. And the half-breed had sworn that O'Malley had pulled out the arrows with his bare hands. That took guts, and for a moment Deane doubted if he could have done it.

He saw Mrs. Grover leave the hotel and wondered why. He noticed the fat drifter coming in along the shady side of the street and carefully noted the details of his dress and the cut of his gun rig, which was low and worn. Gunfighters, he knew, were reluctant to change rigs. An old one was molded to the size and fit of the six-gun and less likely to stick when the draw was made. This man's rig was so old it might full apart at any moment. But when he saw the man stop in front of the Lucky-Seven and tip his hat as he asked Vicky at the door if it was all right to have a cup of coffee, he realized that he was a drifter. A cup of coffee—probably didn't have more than the price of a cup in his jeans, Deane thought, dismissing the man.

The Roberts' wagon was piled high before Silas Grover's store, and the Roberts twins, Paul and Kathy, both eighteen and the oldest of the Roberts kids, were smiling. So Clay Roberts had managed to get a loan out of Vickers. Deane felt a momentary surge of pride in his town and in Vickers, who he knew was overextending himself to make loans to

CALAMITY AT APACHE WELLS

people like Roberts who could offer no more than parched acres and promises in return as security.

Clay Roberts came up with a hundred-pound sack of flour on his shoulder, and Deane stepped up to help him. A moment later, Paul Roberts followed, and the three men wrestled the load to the back of the wagon. Kathy stood to one side, pretty, blonde and happy, holding a brown paper bag. "I won't need any help with this." She held up the bag. "Rock candy for the little ones."

Paul laughed. "If we went home without it, I don't think they'd let us in the house."

"Or they'd set the dogs on us." Clay Roberts laughed. He wrapped his arms around his twins. They were as much alike as two peas in a pod. "Friday, Clint, I'd like to have you come out to the house. I'm getting together all the little fellers like me with burned-out herds an' puttin' a plan to 'em that will combine all the herds into one big one we can drive to Wyomin' fer winter grass. It seems like the only way we kin save what little is left."

Deane nodded that he would be out. Kathy slipped out of her father's arm and stepped away. "Papa, if you don't need me for anything, I'd like to go over to the Lucky-Seven and talk to Miss Vicky. Want to come, Paul?"

"No, thanks, I've heard you and Miss Vicky before. If it ain't cookin', it's sewin'."

"So long, Clay," Deane said. "An' I'm glad you got your loan."

Clint Deane was about to cross the street when he saw Curt Hawkins ride in, stop before the saloon and hitch his bronc to the post. Then Deane saw something that made him wonder. The man was removing his carbine from the saddle boot and walking into the saloon.

Deane forgot about Kid Coxe for a moment and hurried across the street. First one of them goes into the Lucky-Seven, then another shows up and takes his carbine into the Golden Nugget Saloon. For what: to help him fight his way to the bar? Deane snorted to himself.

X

Master Shelby stood before the class and rocked back on his three-inch heels. He knew the children liked it when he wore his gun in the classroom, though he was careful to remove the cartridges. It was a dead gun, but it looked good. "Thomas, I want you to stand up and tell me what year we won our independence."

A sandy-headed boy in the front row stood up. "We won our independence in 1776."

"Correct," Shelby said. "Sit down."

The back door opened before Shelby could ask another question, and Kid Coxe came in quietly, hat in hand, and took a seat in the rear of the room. Everyone turned, and the room began to buzz at the appearance of the stranger. He smiled thinly at Shelby.

"Attention!" Master Shelby demanded in a thunderclap voice. "I want you to meet a former student of mine, when I was teaching back in Lincoln. John Coxe, stand up and show yourself. And just to show you that when I teach you, damn it, you stay taught—John, what was the year that Troy fell to the Greeks?"

Coxe hesitated. And in the schoolroom, his boyish face and slight stature blended in with the others around him. There were several boys in the room larger than Coxe, and if it hadn't been for the gun rig around his middle, he could easily have been taken for a student.

"Stand up, John, when you're asked a question. When did Troy fall to the Greeks?"

Coxe stood up, his face turning crimson. "1184 B.C.," he said softly, and grinned at the kids around him. He sat down. The class applauded wildly.

"See! What did I tell you!" Shelby shouted above the din of noise. But he winked at Coxe, and the gunfighter nodded slightly in response. Both of them knew the other was thinking of the day Shelby had made John Coxe write the date on his copy paper five hundred times as discipline for an infraction of what Shelby loosely called rules.

"In view of the unusual visit by a distinguished scholar, class," Shelby said, "I am going to dismiss you early for recess."

The room broke into bedlam as the children raced for the door. When the last scream and the last body had been squeezed through the door to the school-

CALAMITY AT APACHE WELLS

yard, Shelby walked back to John Coxe. "I ought to make you write, 'I will not disturb the class' two hundred times for coming in here like this, John."

"I'm sorry," Coxe said hurriedly. "I'll leave right now."

"Don't be foolish. Sit down. I couldn't be more pleased. Did you know that you are actually the first and only pupil of mine that ever came back to see me? That's a fact. I've turned out at least five thousand hard-headed roughnecks and another few thousand pretty-faced, stupid females, their little heads chock-full of dates and facts and figures that will never do them much good. But some day, later, when their children have to go to school, they'll remember that it was good here, and they'll send their own precious little bastards to be taught the same useless dates and figures."

Coxe smiled, but only briefly, at the teacher's bitterness and show of cynicism. Actually, he knew that Shelby did not believe what he had said and implied. "You don't mean that, Mistuh Shelby."

"No, I don't, especially after seeing you walk in here. Of all the pupils I could have asked to come back to see me, I'm sure I would have asked for you."

"That's nice of you to say, Mistuh Shelby. But you don't mean it. An' I'm sorry I messed up your teachin'." He stood up to leave.

"Sit down, John, and don't be foolish, or I'll really make you write, 'I will not disturb the class.' "

Coxe sat down, pressing his body around so that the six-gun was free and hanging straight down. Shelby noticed it. "No one will draw on you in here, son," he said.

"I know it," Coxe said. "But it's better not to break a habit. If I don't do it now, I might not do it sometime in the future—an' there I'll be—"

"Gunned without a chance to reach your own weapon," Shelby said.

"Somethin' like that." Coxe got up, walked to the desk at the opposite end of the room and looked at the books. He did not touch them, just looked, blowing the chalk dust off one title; he glanced at Shelby, who watched him, and grinned self-consciously.

"Ever do any more reading?" Shelby asked. He had gone to a closet, had brought out a small basket with his lunch and began spreading a cold half-chicken, a small dish of potato salad, and several apples out on the desk.

"Not any more than a newspaper when I get a hold of one."

"See anything over there you'd like to have?"

"I ain't got the time or the patience any more, Mistuh Shelby," Coxe said, accepting the offered leg of chicken. "I keep on the move a lot."

"Where've you been?"

CALAMITY AT APACHE WELLS 81

"Everywhere, it seems. Me an' my uncle move 'round a lot."

"Where's he now? Here in town with you?"

"No. He'll be 'long directly."

They sat quietly and chewed on the chicken, then turned to the salad and finally sat back with apples. Coxe continued to look frequently at the clock on the wall. It was nearing a quarter past eleven.

"Ever thought about going East, say to Baltimore or New York, and trying to go on with your interest in science, huh, John?"

"Nope. I've been busy."

"Doing what?" Shelby asked.

Coxe looked at him, bringing his eyes up level with the teacher's own face. "Little of this an' that."

"Like bushwhacking and—robbery, maybe?"

"A little."

"Maybe more than a little. Maybe a lot, eh, John?"

"Maybe a lot," Coxe said, and walked around the room again, looking down through the window at the children eating their lunch in the schoolyard.

"You said you were in town on business."

"That's right. I'm gonna rob your bank," Coxe said, and turned to face the immobile face of Master Shelby. "I'm sorry that it has to be your bank. You got any money in it?"

"Not a dime. I couldn't get more than a quarter together to put in it, and that would make me ashamed."

Coxe smiled and nodded. He continued to watch the schoolyard, but beyond the yard was the road north. He kept his eyes on it. He would have to move soon. They would come into town down that road, and he was supposed to have put Deane out of the way. And here he was sitting around talking to a schoolteacher. He moved quickly toward the door. His movement was so fast that it caught Shelby unaware. He made a motion to stop him and was faced suddenly with the sweeping draw of Kid Coxe and the end of his six-gun. The two men stared at each other. Shelby removed his hands and stepped back. Coxe put the gun away. "I'm sorry, but like sittin' down with the rig free, this is a habit, too." He patted the gun after replacing it in the holster.

"Why did you tell me you—"

"That I was gonna rob the bank? Because you can't do anythin' 'bout it," Coxe said.

"I could warn the sheriff."

"I'm goin' lookin' for him now—an' kill him," Coxe said, and a faint smile played at the corners of his mouth. "It'll be self-defense. I won't make a move till he's got his iron clear of leather; then I'll kill him."

"My God!" Shelby said.

"I gotta go now, Mistuh Shelby. It's been nice seein' you again and talkin'. But it's different now.

CALAMITY AT APACHE WELLS 83

I know a lot 'bout things that you don't know anything 'bout."

"I know that you could leave now and go to New York or Philadelphia and go to work and finish your schooling. Some way, somehow, you could continue, if you wanted to."

"It's too late. I got a price on my head."

"Nothing is ever too late."

"What's that you used to call a sayin' like that? A platitude? I don't live with platitudes. I live with my horse an' gun an' the certain knowledge that I'm better'n most men I'll ever see in my lifetime."

"Where do you think it will end?"

"You know where. They'll get me. They'll gang up on me an' trap me some place when my horse throws a shoe or I run up a box canyon, an' then they'll come in an' gun me down." He was not smiling when he talked, and his eyes were hard and frosty, the way Shelby remembered them when John Coxe had come to school with a blackened face after his father had beaten him.

"John, I lied to you. I do have money in the bank. I'll very gladly give it to you if you will promise to go to New York."

"Why?"

"Because I have faith in you."

"No, it's somethin' deeper than that. You're tryin' to protect this town from bein' busted with a run on the bank."

"Party that, but also partly because—"

"Baloney, Mistuh Shelby. Stuff an' nonsense. You ain't got no reason. An' if I had wanted to go on with my lessons, don't you think I would have? I'd have found a way, somehow."

"I won't believe that you deliberately became a gunfighter because of the usual reasons—laziness, cowardice, insanity—"

"No. I found myself runnin' from the law 'cause I killed a man an' I had to protect myself. That's why I am what I am." He moved toward the door.

"Please, John, take the money. I'll walk down to the bank this minute and withdraw it and give it to you."

"No."

"Sheriff Deane will—the man you think you're going to kill will kill you. I've seen him in a gun fight. He's as fast as you are."

"No, he ain't," Coxe said. "No, he ain't as fast as me."

"What makes you think so? You've never seen him, or have you?"

"Never set eyes on him. But he wants to live, an' I don't give a damn."

"You don't mean that."

"I do, Mistuh Shelby. I surely do."

He stepped through the door.

XI

Kid Coxe walked out of the schoolyard and down the middle of the main street until there were buildings, and then he stepped up onto the boardwalk. He walked slowly, his hands loose beside his hips, his hat pushed back a little. He passed the Lucky-Seven, and Grady Potts nodded slightly, jerking his head in the direction of the saloon, which he had seen Clint Deane enter after leaving the restaurant.

Deane spotted the young man quickly. There was something meaningful about the way the quiet youth was walking. When Deane saw him move off the boardwalk down into the street and start toward him, he knew what was coming. He set his hat firmly on his head, eased the six-gun in the holster and stepped out of the shade into the brilliant sunshine. He marched toward Kid Coxe slowly, carefully, watching the man's right shoulder.

Sheriff Deane became aware that people were crowding the boardwalk. He wanted to tell them to get back inside and stay out of the way, but did not dare take his eyes off the approaching Kid Coxe.

They were seventy-five feet apart. Deane continued walking, and Kid Coxe suddenly came to a standstill. "Your name John Coxe, sometimes called Kid?" Deane demanded in a loud vibrant voice that crackled with authority.

Coxe was silent.

Along the boardwalk, Grady Potts moved through the crowd, still holding his cup of coffee, his eyes sharp and bright as he watched the two men.

"Answer my question!" demanded Deane.

Kid Coxe did not reply. He kept his eyes glued on Deane's face.

And then something happened. Deane was to say later that he thought the world had come to a standstill when he heard the screams of the Indians and the rapid fire of a six-gun squeezed off up near the schoolyard.

He had not taken his eyes off Kid Coxe, but the murmur of those crowded on the boardwalk became loud, and there was a movement toward the school.

Deane hesitated, but not for long. He was a lawman, and Kid Coxe was wanted. But he was also sheriff of Apache Wells, and in that respect his duty was to the people of that town. The shots had come from the school area. The crowd was moving. He stared at Coxe. "Get out of town. If you're not gone

CALAMITY AT APACHE WELLS 87

by noon, I'm comin' to get you."

Kid Coxe had not moved and had not taken his eyes from Deane.

Clint Deane moved quickly when he turned away from Kid Coxe. And what he saw in the brief instant would remain with him until his last day. He glanced northward toward the mountains. Kathy Roberts was about to cross the street toward the Lucky-Seven. Clay Roberts and his son Paul had stopped loading the wagon and were now shoving the hundred-pound sack of flour into the back. Seeing Deane break off from facing Coxe, they turned their attention toward the schoolyard. Douglas Vickers had taken a few snorts in the saloon and had been heading back to his bank, not paying the slightest attention to the two gunmen in the street, but he stopped now to look toward the schoolyard. And Deane saw Grady Potts drinking a cup of coffee, though he did not know the man's name. Doc Marlowe was approaching the saloon from his right, talking to himself, some of the woman's blood still on his shirtsleeves where it had spurted.

The riders drifting up the street, who had pulled over to one side to watch Coxe and Deane, the few wagons, the knot of cattlemen and loafers around the spring became still. And all of it, Deane was to say later, stopped dead.

And then the Indian war party came. The street

was full of them. Apache Wells boasted a wider street than the usual town because of the occasional herds which passed through, headed toward the northern markets. But the full breadth was filled with screaming, painted Indians. They made a single pass from the school to the opposite end of town and then turned back again.

The crowded boardwalk, which ordinarily would have been empty except for a few people moving about from store to store, settling down against the hard three-hour fight against the afternoon heat from one to four, was a milling mob of screaming men, women and children. The men began to fire back at the Indians. The women began to pull the children into the stores.

Somehow Kathy Roberts had gotten trapped in the middle of the street when she attempted to get back to her father and brother. Deane saw Clay Roberts fall to the ground, a shaft in his chest. And then Deane came alive. He must have screamed, though later he denied it when the men in the saloon said they had never heard anything like it before. He pulled his six-gun and stepped back into the street, leveled it and began firing. Other shots began to pour into the surge of Indians as they raced from one end of town to the other, firing their arrows and carbines from the sides of their ponies as they ducked and bobbed and weaved but never wavered in their attack.

CALAMITY AT APACHE WELLS

And then Kathy Roberts was swept up in the dust of the hooves. And Deane saw her jerked clear of the ground and swung to the back of the pony of the leading Indian brave, all in one motion, at breakneck speed. The Indians made a final turn up and down the street and began to withdraw. By now the men in the saloon and the shopkeepers were blasting away with shotguns. Indians began to fall from their mounts, and the ponies began to stumble as they were hit with the heavy guns that were now leveled at the throng. It was impossible to miss. You just aimed your piece at the herd and fired, and something fell.

But it was not enough. More than half of them blew unscathed through the town like a big violent wind, pounded down past the livery stable and kept on going.

Sheriff Clint Deane stood in the middle of the street, inserting cartridges into his six-gun as fast as he could. Around him he could hear the screams of the wounded and the dying, the frightened and the brave. The street which usually reflected the peaceful life, looked as if it had been struck by a heavy hand in three dozen places at the same time. The Roberts' team of horses lay dead, the wagon overturned. The flour, spilling into the street, was trampled. Clay Roberts was stretched out on the boardwalk with the shaft sticking straight up out of his chest.

Behind him, Doc Marlowe was sitting peacefully in a chair, smiling foolishly as he looked down at the blood pouring out of his stomach, and then Deane saw him relax and go limp in the stillness of death.

Paul Roberts was screaming and running down the middle of the street, shooting a six-gun, though the Indians had disappeared. Someone ran out and grabbed him and knocked him cold with a pistol butt. Mrs. Grover was moaning and crying, down on her hands and knees beside her husband, who was streaming blood from a superficial scalp wound and trying desperately to push his wife away.

Several of the men, among whom Deane recognized Douglas Vickers the banker, a man opposed to violence, were running from Indian to Indian, putting a bullet in each downed brave's head.

Vicky Deane came running along the edge of the boardwalk, the rider in back of her still carrying his cup of coffee in one hand, a sweet roll in the other.

"They took Kathy Roberts!" someone yelled. And Deane's head cleared.

And then, if the town had stood still the moment the Indians swept through, it came alive now. Men began to run toward the livery and the horses that had been torn loose from the hitching rails. They began to trail out of the town after the Indian party, alone and in groups of two's and three's. Deane

CALAMITY AT APACHE WELLS

found that someone had taken his black, and he turned to the first horse in the stalls—Kid Coxe's black stallion. The animal came to life at the touch of his hand and was out of the stable at a dead gallop in two full strides; Deane had never ridden such an animal before. He turned to see that more than half of the men in Apache Wells were mounted and pounding after him. He saw ahead of him the dust of those that had gotten out first, but on the big stallion it was not too long before he had overtaken them and passed them. Each man was intent, a furious, insane hatred on his face.

The land was flat, and there was no mistaking which way the Indians had gone. A half-mile out of town, Deane passed the shaft-riddled body of Alex Mayer, who had been unlucky enough to round a turn in the trail and face the band of insane savages. He had been hit nine times, all of them in the chest or head, and he had died before he hit the ground.

Deane did not know who the rider was and did not care. The Indians were ahead of him, and they had Kathy Roberts. And they had disrupted his town, had killed a lot of his people, and it was his job to hunt them down.

XII

Austin Bailey and Todd Bain rode into Apache Wells, evading the fallen bodies of the Indians and the townfolk and the dead carcasses of the Indian horses, looking at them without feeling or emotion. Mrs. Grover hailed them, croaking weakly, "You men! We've got to have some help—someone has to ride to Shiprock—"

Bailey and Bain turned their heads to look at Mrs. Grover without expression. They did not stop their broncs, who were slowly weaving in and out of the littered street.

"Men—" Mrs. Grover cried tearfully.

Neither of them turned to look at her again. They came to the still unconscious body of Paul Roberts, his face in the dirt where he had fallen. They examined it with experienced eyes and saw that he was still alive, but they did not stop. They moved on past the body of Clay Roberts, past the store. Mrs. Grover hurried into the store, where she stopped screaming and began taking care of her husband.

CALAMITY AT APACHE WELLS 93

At the saloon, they wheeled their ponies to the hitch rail and slipped off to the ground, careful not to step on the outstretched body of a dead Indian, and then walked into the saloon, which was empty except for Curt Hawkins.

"Looks like there might have been some dingdong doings," Austin Bailey said, and walked to the bar.

"Never saw so many dead people at one time in my life," Todd Bain said. Both Bailey and Bain drank from a bottle, while Hawkins moved to the door and looked out.

All three men stood at the door, shaded by the shadows, and watched the movement in the street as the living worked their way among the dead and wounded, searching for those who might still live. None of the three men said a word but watched silently. Finally it was Bain who turned away from the door and ambled in back of the bar and found the cash box. He emptied it slowly, counting the bills. Bailey and Hawkins returned to the bar and watched him.

"How much?" Bailey asked.

"Near two hundred dollars," Bain said with a slow smile. He shoved the money into his pocket.

A ten-year-old boy banged the batwing doors open, and the three men moved like one. They had their six-guns out, cocked and leveled at the wide-eyed

94 CALAMITY AT APACHE WELLS

lad before he could open his mouth.

"What do you want, boy?" Bailey demanded, and put his gun away. Bain and Hawkins slipped their irons into leather.

"I been told to find every able-bodied man in Apache Wells an' have all of 'em come to help with the wounded."

"Okay, boy. We'll be along," Bailey said.

"Now git!" Bain said.

"Yessuh!"

The doors swung to and fro when the boy let go of them, and the three men leaned against the bar facing the street, some of which was visible to them through the windows. "I was in a town in Montana that was hit by Injuns like this when I was a kid," Hawkins said. "Lost two brothers."

"I know. It's a devilish thing for them Injuns to come sweepin' in like this without no warnin'," Bain remarked.

"Soldiers more'n likely will follow this one up. I'll bet anything the soldiers will chase these Indians right down to and through the Pacific Ocean," Hawkins said.

"Wonder what happened to Kid Coxe, Grady an' Alex," Bailey said, changing the subject.

"I seen Grady down at the Lucky-Seven a minute 'fore the whole town ran after the Injuns. I don't know if he got on his bronc an' lit out with the others

CALAMITY AT APACHE WELLS   95

or not. I know I almost did. I think every man who could fork a horse must be out cuttin' fer the southwest," Hawkins said, and spat on the floor. He still carried his carbine. He had not fired a single shot in defense of Apache Wells.

"Where you reckon Alex is?" Bain asked.

"I'd say he's dead," Hawkins said, rejoining them at the bar. "We all came up the south trail, an' that's the way the Injuns left. He would have been right in their path."

Bailey and Bain looked at each other, and neither of them showed any expression on their faces.

"Did Kid Coxe down that lawman?" Bailey asked.

"No, he didn't. I ain't seen him. But I saw Deane. He was standin' right outside the door yonder when the Injuns made their run through town." He glanced at the clock over the bar. "But he still has plenty of time. It ain't but eleven-thirty. We said we wouldn't be in till eleven-thirty-five."

"Well," Bailey said, "might as well go on down to the bank an' make a withdrawal."

They wheeled out of the saloon onto the boardwalk. A few people were moving around now—women and old men. They were moving among the dead in the street, examining them carefully, hopeful that some of them might still be alive. They carried Paul Roberts into the Grover store, and the still breathing body of O'Malley, who had torn the bandages off his hands and tried to fire a shotgun. There was an arrow in his stomach, and they didn't expect him to live, but they took him inside out of the sun.

Bailey saw Grady Potts first. The body of their partner was wedged in between the bodies of two Indian pintos and slammed up against the side of the boardwalk. The crush of the blow as he fell backward had snapped the man's neck on the cottonwood planking of the boardwalk. He still held the coffee cup.

Bailey stopped and looked into the quiet face. "I told him not to get anything but a cup of coffee."

They moved on. The stillness of the scene affected them but did not move them, because they did not know these people and did not care about them; the Indians were not considered at all.

"Let's get the cash an' get the hell outa here," Bailey said.

"Yup. This place is beginning to get on my nerves, too," Bain said.

"Well, here's the bank," Hawkins remarked.

Vicky Deane was in the Grover store, working over the boy who had died two minutes before. She continued to wash the wound in the boy's head and was preparing to bandage it when she noticed the wound wasn't bleeding any more. She was so dazed she did not react. She simply dropped the bandage to the

CALAMITY AT APACHE WELLS   97

floor and turned to another who lay moaning at her feet.

The half-breed driver was there, helping, sweating, talking, and doing things that Mrs. Grover and the other women could not do: cauterizing muscle wounds, binding a wound tight in its own blood, pulling heavy supply bins out of the way for more floor space. No one knew who had selected the general store as a medical station. The saloon would have been much better, but no one realized this. The town's organization had fallen apart; it was unable to move. Life was there, it functioned, but it had no inner, directed action. The people moved as if asleep. No one had even considered a second attack.

Vicky Deane was one of the first to come out of this paralysis. The color had drained out of her when she had seen Kathy Roberts swept to the back of the Indian pony; when she had seen men dropping to the ground; when she had seen Doc Marlowe so still in death and realized that the only medical aid in town was gone.

But now her senses came back—hard and fast, so fast that it was as if a blow had been struck on the back of her head. Her head began to ache, and she gasped for breath.

"We need help," she said quietly to the half-breed.

"No men in town," the man replied. "All dead,

or go—" he made an Indian sign— "after Indians."

"There must be someone in town who can help us. We've got to get these people into beds and have their wounds taken care of."

"You want Big Foot go to Shiprock?" the half-breed asked.

"Yes, go to Shiprock. Tell them we need help—and quickly."

The half-breed was three strides out of the door. "And bring the doctor!" Vicky Deane said. "Doc Marlowe is dead."

"You got doctor—little boy help Doc Marlowe this mornin'."

"What boy?"

"No name." Big Foot was on a horse. "He mebbe so dead, too."

"Hurry," Vicky Deane said. "Bring back help."

The half-breed whipped the saddle bronc with a furious snap of the trailing reins, so hard that the animal shuddered, then, as if on springs, shot forward down the edge of the street and to the southwest.

And then, out of the dark shadows on the shady side of the street, Master Shelby strode—or was he running?—toward Vicky Deane.

"Oh, thank God!"

Vicky Deane saw the street swimming before her, and then felt the strong fingers of Master Shelby biting into her flesh as he caught her from fainting.

CALAMITY AT APACHE WELLS 99

"We'd better hurry," Shelby said to Kid Coxe, who stepped out from behind the big schoolteacher.

But Kid Coxe saw something else at that moment. There was no mistaking Austin Bailey's horse before the saloon. And the one next to it belonged to Todd Bain.

He hesitated. "Come on, John!" Shelby demanded.

Kid Coxe still did not move. He studied the stores and the windows on the opposite side of the street, his eye traveling beyond the dead in the dust to the bank. Was that movement inside the bank? He wasn't sure.

Shelby spun the youth around and slapped him across the face. "You're not going to rob that bank and walk out on these people!"

It was the first time anyone had touched Kid Coxe since the last time his father had struck him and Coxe had killed him with a shotgun at the age of thirteen. The six-gun was in his hand, and he was pulling down on the trigger when his vision cleared from the blurred red the sting of the slap had provoked, and he saw Shelby striding into the store with Vicky Deane in his arms.

Kid Coxe turned to look at the bank. He saw Austin Bailey and Todd Bain through the glass.

Shelby was at the door, his gun in his hand and aimed at John Coxe. "Either you come in and help these people, or I'll kill you."

Coxe saw Hawkins in the doorway of the bank. And then Hawkins saw him. The man waved and turned to speak to Bailey and Bain still inside the bank.

Bailey stepped guardedly toward the door and then back quickly. Hawkins also jumped back inside. A moment later, Bain inched Hawkins' carbine around the edge of the door frame and aimed at Kid Coxe.

"Are you going to move?" Shelby demanded.

Bain fired just as Coxe dropped to his left and brought up his six-gun. Shelby, thinking the man in the bank was shooting at him to protect Coxe, squeezed the trigger. The hammer fell dead on one of the empty cartridges.

"Get back!" Coxe shouted, diving for protection behind the carcass of an Indian pony. Bain fired again, and Shelby saw the men were shooting at Coxe. He jumped back inside the store.

He closed his eyes tight. The world was going mad. This was the end of the world. This wasn't a real day. It was a dream. At any minute he expected to wake up.

But the sudden screams of a cattleman, one of those trapped near the spring, brought him back to reality. He turned, ignoring the sharp whine of the solitary carbine shots outside, and began doing what he could for the men on the floor.

XIII

Kathy Roberts saw immediately that it would be foolish to try to resist the Indian while they were riding. Her time would have to come later. She could slip from the back of the Indian pony easily enough, but there were those in back of her to catch her the moment she put her foot on the ground, even if she escaped the pounding hoofs, which was not likely.

She clung to the waist of the Indian, nestling up close to him, laying her cheek on his back and hugging him for dear life. She could smell his strong body odor, and her hands had begun to slip a little from the war paint the Indian had smeared on his chest.

The trail ended, and they were out in open range country. From the direction of the party, she knew they were heading for the mountains. She turned and dared a glance over her shoulder to see if they were being pursued, but she could see nothing but the faces of the Indians behind her.

Kathy Roberts was a clear-headed girl. She had not been mother to the Roberts' brood for over three years without learning a certain degree of patience and the advantage of compromise. Whatever was ahead of her, Kathy thought, she would do what was necessary to live.

The Indian before her on the pony suddenly screamed and raised his hand. But they did not change their direction, nor did anything happen behind her that she could see. It was just a scream of triumph—and somehow its meaning penetrated the barrier between red and white, and Kathy Roberts, for all her courage, felt an icy breath blow in her face.

Clint Deane had ridden out over the flats, leaving the others behind him. He was already within sight of the dust the Indian party had raised and felt pretty confident that nothing would happen to Kathy Roberts as long as they were on the move. He checked the big stallion slightly and glanced back at the onrushing, laboring crowd behind him. The Indians were out on the open range, and they would be easy to follow; their rising dust would be visible for miles.

Still moving fast but not at a dead run, he allowed the others to catch up with him. The first, red-faced and sweaty, breathing hard, was Douglas

CALAMITY AT APACHE WELLS 103

Vickers. Vickers was riding Deane's horse, but it was unimportant now, and Deane would not have given up Kid Coxe's stallion at the moment for anything in the country. In this pursuit he would need a good horse, and the stallion was the finest piece of horseflesh he had ever straddled.

"We can't all go tearin' off after 'em!" Deane shouted to the others. "They tore up the town, an' back there people are gonna need some help."

"I don't give a damn 'bout anything but gettin' that bunch of Indians yonder," a tall, hard-eyed young man said.

"You'll do as I say!" Deane said suddenly, his temper blowing.

"Talk to the others, mister, but Apache Wells ain't my town. I come from Shiprock."

"He's O'Malley's brother," Vickers said. "I'll go back to town, Clint. You're right. I couldn't do much more than be in the way. I don't know what came over me to do what I've done. But I guess I went crazy for a spell."

"No need to say anything, Mister Vickers," Deane said. "I seen Doc Marlowe git it, an there ain't nobody that kin take care of the wounded—" he stopped "—except maybe that young stranger that helped the doc when the stage arrived. He goes by the name of Kid Coxe."

"I'll go back," Vickers said. He swung his pony

around to the others. It looked as if every man and boy in Apache Wells had found a horse and streaked out of town after the Indians. "Most of you men had better come with me. You, Ted Grover, and Smuthers —you ain't any better at Indian fightin' than I am. We'd better go back where we can do some good."

"One of you men on a good horse ride to Shiprock right now and get some help," Deane said. And before he had finished speaking, two youngsters had cut loose from the group and pounded their saddles, whipping their mounts hard.

"I don't think we'll ever corner 'em an' get the savage rascals to fight," Deane said. "They're headin' fer their village. Only chance we got of gettin' Kathy Roberts back—" Deane realized by the expressions on their faces that most of them did not know the Indians had taken the girl. They began to shout and curse.

"Shut up! Damn it! Now be quiet!" Deane commanded.

Vickers had already moved to Smuthers and Grover, preparing to ride back to Apache Wells, but the others wanted to go on. There wasn't one in the group of fifty who didn't know and have a feeling of special warmth for Kathy Roberts, who was taking care of her little brothers and sisters.

It was all Deane could do to shout them down and keep them from riding off after the rapidly disap-

CALAMITY AT APACHE WELLS 105

pearing dust of the Indian party. "I'll get Kathy Roberts back, and I'll bring back enough Indian scalps to make even the maddest of you satisfied. But dammit, we can't run with an army 'cross them flats without water or anything to fight with. I kin see from here that half of you ain't got guns, an' ain't but a few of you got carbines—which is what we'll need to fight 'em with."

Vickers and Grover and Smuthers had already turned away. There was no use talking. They were needed back in Apache Wells. It was the moment Deane had hoped for. The men turned and saw the older men headed back toward town, and Deane seized the opportunity to chase most of them back. "I ain't gonna let any man come along that ain't got a six-gun and a carbine!" he shouted.

They didn't like to be talked to that way. Their lives had been threatened, their property destroyed, and friends and relatives lay dead or near dying. "I'm gonna go!" said a man near Deane.

Clint Deane did not hesitate. He drew his six-gun and rammed it into the man's stomach. "I said you ain't. I ain't gonna jeopardize Kathy Roberts an' the chances of gettin' her back 'cause some damn fool is hard-headed."

There was the slightest hesitation, and Deane knew they might turn him aside and ride on, hellbent for leather, into the open range and try to shoot it out with the Apaches, in which case the first thing the Indians would do would be to cut Kathy Roberts' throat."

"All right," Deane shouted. "Now that you understand me, every man here that's got a carbine, a six-gun an' a canteen full of water, move over on this side."

"You ain't got no canteen of water," someone shouted.

"I don't need water," Deane said harshly.

Seven men rode to Deane's side, and he checked their saddle boots and their six-guns before he allowed they could ride with him. "Now the rest of you get back to town an' help them people. There ain't one of you thought 'bout the schoolhouse full of kids, an' that the Indians had to pass the schoolyard 'fore they come to town."

"That's right," a voice shouted.

"Sheriff's tellin' it straight," someone else agreed.

"I plumb forgot 'bout them young uns," still another voice said.

And then they turned in a group and pounded after Vickers, Grover and Smuthers.

Deane turned to the seven. "They won't make it back to their village—if I'm right in thinkin' they're tryin' to get back there an' right in thinkin' the village is in the mountains. They're goin' to have to make camp sometime tonight, an' that's when we'll

CALAMITY AT APACHE WELLS 107

hit 'em."

Most of the men were young, and Deane was glad of that. They would be easier to control, and they would have a better chance of winning, not needing water or food as badly as older men who did not have their energy. The oldest of the group was the man Vickers had said was O'Malley's brother. Deane saw that the man resembled O'Malley strongly. "You ain't got a six-gun," Deane accused him.

"No, I ain't. But I'll out-gun any man alive with this carbine," the man replied.

"I ain't got time to argue. An' you'll get a chance to prove what you say. All right; let's move out. We'll take it slow and easy, 'cause to run the horses 'cross that dry rangeland will be askin' for 'em to give out on us."

The eight riders turned as a group and started after the Indian party to the west and a little south, riding at a fast trot, eyes scanning the sky for signs of dust. They did not see any more dust of the Indians, but these men did not need a cloud of dust to tell them where the Indians had gone. They could, each of them, read the signs in the hard, trackless ground as if there were signposts dug into the earth.

Deane was riding alone, a few feet out in front of the others, when O'Malley's brother came alongside him. "This is Spotted Pony we're huntin', you know."

"What's your name?" Deane demanded.

"Patrick O'Malley, An' I s'pose you're the hard-tailed lawman they call Clint Deane?"

"I am."

"Glad to meet you, lawman," Patrick O'Malley said.

"How do you know it's Spotted Pony?"

"Same one that attacked the stage. Foster told me."

"Who told you?"

"My brother. You used his last name—O'Malley—that's the family name. I reckon it's good fer you that you didn't know 'bout his first name. You might've had a helluva fight if'n you'd called him Foster. I did oncet, when we were shavers over south of Shiprock, an' he whupped me so bad I didn't chew fer a week."

"You know anything 'bout Spotted Pony?"

Patrick O'Malley was silent a moment. "Nothin' too much, but a little here an' there. Jest talk. I heard a buffalo hide man say that he passed through Spotted Pony's village a spell back to do some tradin' an' heard a lot of talk 'bout Spotted Pony actin' up 'gainst the old chief. Could be that a young buck like Spotted Pony got some followers together an' they jes' rode 'round the countryside raisin' hell."

"Which would explain why they come in shootin' up an' down the main street like they did, without

CALAMITY AT APACHE WELLS 109

stoppin' to lift anybody's hair," Deane said.

"Well, leastwise not anyone that we know 'bout," O'Malley said slowly.

"Meanin' what?"

"This Kathy Roberts has got hair, ain't she?" O'Malley asked.

Spotted Pony was jubilant. His scouts had just told him the white eyes had split up, and the biggest part of them had returned to their village. Only eight of them followed now, and they were not running their ponies hard.

The braves looked upon their leader respectfully. He had burned his medicine, had led them into the white village of Apache Wells, and from the way Spotted Pony received the news of the eight that were following, they knew that something was soon to be decided.

The Indian leader slipped from his horse and stood on the ground. He studied the ground and the surrounding countryside. He turned to look at the faces of the others. There was some hesitation. Spotted Pony turned suddenly, pulled Kathy Roberts from the back of the pony and held her by the wrists. The girl looked at him, eyes defiant, but she said nothing. The others crowded around to see what Spotted Pony was going to do. Suddenly the Indian grabbed the top of her cotton dress and ripped it from her shoulders. The full, firm white breasts quivered. The Indians spoke to each other, murmuring. Spotted Pony held her wrists and looked at her, then spoke to the others. Then he ripped the rest of the dress from the girl's body. Kathy did not move. She watched the Indian standing before her speak rapidly to the others, and waited.

Spotted Pony stepped forward, grabbed Kathy around the waist and put her on his pony; then he slipped up behind her. He screamed at the others, and they began to ride again across the flats to the distant low mesa where Spotted Pony had told them they would lay the trap and catch the white eyes.

XIV

Kid Coxe remained behind the body of the dead Indian pony and watched the door of the bank. Todd Bain appeared again, his eye squinting down the barrel of a carbine, and fired. The slug tore into the leg of the dead horse, and Coxe remained still. Bain fired again, and then again. He stuck his head out a little further, cautiously, and that was when Kid Coxe brought the sixgun up and fired. He heard Bain yell and jerk back, but in the instant following the shot, he knew he had only creased the man in the bank doorway.

Behind him Shelby saw what was going on, but it made little sense to him. He dismissed the firing from his mind as if brushing away the annoyance of a fly buzzing around his head.

Inside the bank, Bain was holding his ear. "Damned Kid shot my ear off!" he screamed.

"Shut up!" Austin Bailey said. "Get the gun, Hawkins, an' finish that slimy bastard."

"What fer? I thought he was part of—"

Hawkins didn't get a chance to finish. Austin Bailey drew his six-gun and fired into the man's chest, then turned away before Hawkins hit the floor.

"Tie your head up with this," Bailey said to Bain, "an' shut off that bellyaching." He handed over his neckerchief.

"Git him! Austin, fer God's sake, git him," Bain pleaded.

"I'll git him."

He stepped to the door with the carbine and looked out into the street. Men were running, bent over, from doorway to doorway, skittering along in the shadows of the boardwalk, but Bailey did not see Kid Coxe.

"Let's get out of here," he said to Bain. They started for the back of the bank, picking up the two small valises in which they had stuffed the money, and hurried to the back door. They opened the door cautiously and then moved quickly down the alley in back of the stores toward the saloon and their horses. They rounded a corner leading to the main street and stopped dead still. A woman was walking slowly, carrying the limp body of a child in her arms. There was no indication how the child had been injured, but there was doubt that the child was still alive.

CALAMITY AT APACHE WELLS 113

Once the woman had passed, they slipped out of the corner shadows and hurried to the edge of the building and the main street.

The pair peered around the corner cautiously. There was movement in the street now. Shelby and Vicky Deane were moving among the dead, looking for more wounded. Mrs. Grover was close to them and stopped, dropping to her knees beside the limp body of a man. "I think this one's still alive!" she shouted.

Shelby and Vicky Deane turned to Mrs. Grover, and from the sides of the buildings, moving cautiously, others entered into the openness of the street.

"Come on, while they're messin' 'round out there!" Austin Bailey said. The two men slipped out of the alley and made for their horses.

Bain held his six-gun in one hand and pressed the neckerchief to his bleeding ear with the other. Bailey carried the valises. They swung up on their horses quickly and turned them away from the railing.

Kid Coxe had followed them through the bank, past the dead body of Hawkins and into the alley. He came around the corner just as they were breaking down the street. He fired once and missed, fired again, but by then they were out of range. The group in the street around Shelby, Vicky Deane and Mrs. Grover turned at the gunshots and saw Kid Coxe standing alone, taking careful aim after the retreating riders, but they did not know what it was all about. Except Shelby. He watched through the thick, dulling fog of his senses that a near massacre in Apache Wells had brought down over his mind, and he understood that Kid Coxe was trying to stop the men. "It's all right," he said quietly. "Everything's being taken care of."

But Kid Coxe missed as the riders moved out of range. He turned and ran into the shade of the boardwalk. The store was too crowded now.

"We'll need something to keep these wounds clean," he said to one of the men nearby. "Go over to the saloon and get some whiskey."

The man nodded and hurried across the street. When he entered the Golden Nugget saloon, he noticed the clock on the wall over the bar. Exactly twelve o'clock. It had been only forty minutes since the Indians had swept through Apache Wells. And it seemed like forty hours. He ran back across the street with the liquor.

Kid Coxe found a horse two blocks away. A woman came to the back of the house and watched him come into the yard, where the horse was swishing his tail. "You can't take that animal!" she screamed. "I've got to get my baby to the doctor in Shiprock!"

Kid Coxe looked up. The woman was holding a child in her arms. He walked to her side. "Ma'am, ain't nothin' can be done fer this young un. It's dead."

He saw that the head had been crushed by a heavy blow. The woman said, "I ain't gonna let you take that horse. I'm gettin' ready now to take my baby to the doctor in Shiprock. If you wanted to help a poor woman, you could hitch up the buckboard."

Kid Coxe tried to take the dead child out of her arms, but the woman would not let go. He stepped back. "I'm sorry, ma'am, but I need that horse." He hurried to the barn, found a saddle and began leading the horse into the shade.

The woman appeared at the back door of the house without the child. Instead, she carried a shotgun. Kid Coxe pulled the horse around the edge of the barn door just as the woman fired. Then, without warning, she fired a second time, point-blank into the side of the barn. Kid Coxe stepped into the stirrup and lashed the horse hard across the rump with trailing reins. The animal leaped out of the barn door and was through the yard before the woman could break the gun and reload. She stood a long time looking after Kid Coxe, and then she went back into the house and began laying out clothes for the trip to Shiprock. "Never you mind, honey; Mama's gonna see that you're all right," she said to the motionless child on the bed.

XV

Because he knew how to organize things, Douglas Vickers took over the cleaning up of the main street of Apache Wells. The dead numbered twelve; the wounded, ten. Nine horses, one mule and five wagons had been destroyed. Nine of the Indians had been killed, and five of their ponies. They removed the wounded to the saloon and the dead to the livery stable because it was the coolest place in town. The Indians were dragged by their heels through the dust at the end of a rope and dumped without comment or ceremony in a hastily dug communal hole half a mile outside of town. The horses were dragged to the flats, soaked with coal oil and set afire. Vickers worked tirelessly, and as much of his effort went into consoling the widowed women who had lost husbands and the mothers who had lost sons as into attempting to get Apache Wells back on its feet.

It wasn't until two o'clock in the afternoon, when the street began to resemble its former dusty but

CALAMITY AT APACHE WELLS 117

neat self, that Vickers went to the bank and found the dead body of Hawkins and the empty safe.

Douglas Vickers was a strong man. His mind was clear, and he held to his opinions, which were usually founded in common sense, a fear of God and a love for his fellow man. But when he saw the empty safe and the more than seventy-seven thousand dollars in cash missing, he knew that there wasn't much use trying to keep the town together. The past two years had been too much for him. It seemed that he alone had been holding the spirit of Apache Wells together with his loan from a Denver bank. Now the floodgates had been opened.

He sat down behind his desk and wiped the sweat from his eyes. It was just as well, he thought, that the bank had been robbed. After today, seventy-seven thousand dollars would be a drop in the bucket compared to what the town's needs were going to be once the damages had been totaled. He thought about Clay Roberts and the loan he had made to the man early that morning. Vickers did not want to take over Roberts' spread or his mangy cattle. He wanted Clay Roberts alive to work the spread and keep his cattle alive, and in turn to pay back the loan. Of course there was the boy, Paul, but what would he do when he learned that his sister had been taken by the Indians? Grab a gun and go off looking for a killing. And that would leave Roberts kids and the Roberts' spread to be defaulted to the bank. And the bank didn't want it.

At least, in the Roberts' case, there was the possibility that Paul would take over. But what of the families of the others that had been killed in the slashing attack by the Apaches?

Shelby came in to help remove the body of Hawkins and saw the banker, curiously detached, sitting behind the desk as if he were deliberating a loan to a rancher. Shelby let the others take the body away and walked to the man's side. "What's the matter, Douglas? You look like you don't believe any of it. Well, take it from me, it's true."

"They robbed the bank," Vickers said quietly.

"I know they did. I couldn't stop them—" Shelby said. He remembered Kid Coxe shooting at the men in the bank and wondered if the youth had killed the man they had just removed from the bank floor. "I tried, but I couldn't think."

"You know what that means to Apache Wells?" Vickers inquired.

"I have an idea."

"We're finished. It wipes me out. That trip I made to Denver this spring was for a loan—all of it on my personal property."

Shelby stared through the windows, where the last of the Indian ponies were being dragged away to the flats by the sweating red-eyed men of the town.

CALAMITY AT APACHE WELLS 119

"There isn't a family in Apache Wells—or near it—that won't take a loss today, either through the failure of the bank or the personal loss of having someone killed. You might as well pack your bags and leave now. This town is dead."

Whether the town of Apache Wells was dead or not, Master Shelby thought, depended entirely upon one's point of view. He walked the side of the street toward the saloon, needing a drink badly, forgetting for the moment that it had been converted into a medical station. He knew that he shouldn't be bothering about liquor at this time, but he was shaking, and he knew that he had been shaking since early that morning. And the cause of this inner tension, he knew, was not the Indian attack, or the sight and sound and smell of the dead and dying, but his sudden encounter with Kid Coxe.

He wondered now about the shooting that had taken place between the men inside the bank and Coxe. Had he convinced Coxe, in his talk in the schoolroom a few minutes before the Indians attacked full force? Was it fuzzy-mindedness on his part to believe, to want to believe that Coxe had tried to stop the robbery when he had so coolly demonstrated that there was nothing Shelby could do to stop it, and that he was in fact gunning for Deane, who might be the one person in Apache Wells who could stop the bank robbery? He wondered about the little boy back in Lincoln who had wanted to be a doctor. Was this the first time that anyone had ever talked sympathetically to him since those days when he was a student of Shelby's? And had there been a reaction when Shelby had offered to withdraw the little money he had in the Apache Wells Bank and give it to him? Had Coxe understood that he was not trying to bribe him not to rob the bank, but sincerely wanted him to put a halt to one way of life and begin another?

Shelby stopped before the door of the saloon, deep in thought, his eyes studying the distance where the men had ridden out of Apache Wells with the money, and decided that Apache Wells would indeed be finished if John "Kid" Coxe did not come back with the money.

"Scuse me, Mistah Shelby, but Miss Vicky needs you inside." A young boy stood at his side.

Shelby nodded and stepped into the saloon. Whether Douglas Vickers was right or wrong depended entirely, Shelby saw with crushing clarity, on what John "Kid" Coxe did or did not do.

Vicky Deane, when Shelby had taken over in the Golden Nugget Saloon, had found renewed strength when she woke from the dead faint and with clear-headedness knew exactly what she should do. Mrs. Grover and several other women were handling the wounded; there was nothing she could do there that

CALAMITY AT APACHE WELLS 121

would be more important than doing what she knew best: preparing food. She left the saloon as the men rode back into town and began cleaning out the dead and wounded.

Once inside the Lucky-Seven Restaurant, the first time she had had a moment to herself since the Indians had passed through the town, she leaned against the door and closed her eyes. She was tired, but she was sure about what she had to do. She found the cook sitting placidly beside the stove, the full dinner prepared as if waiting for diners to enter the Lucky-Seven and begin sending in their orders. "We've got to cook more," she said, and the cook nodded. "This town has gone crazy today, absolutely mad. But mad or not, people are going to be hungry. Take the biggest pot and make coffee—no, take the two biggest pots. And bread—I'll start mixing corn-meal dough for cornbread. Is there any more of the calf's quarter left?"

The cook nodded.

"We'll stew it. There isn't going to be a thing cooked in this town for twenty-four hours, the way things are, and I'm going to have to feed two hundred hungry people. And there isn't anybody to help us."

"*Si.*"

"Have you been here all the time?"

"*Si,*" the old cook said.

"What have you been doing?"

"Preparing the calf, *señorita*. I know people must eat before the *señorita* come and tell me."

Vicky frowned. "I don't understand."

"In my country, many times the villages and towns were raided like this town, and always when the fighting was over, the people forgot about food and there wasn't anything to eat. The corn-meal dough is ready, *señorita;* I am waiting now for it to set for a while before putting it into the oven. The coffee is ready. If you will get one of the men, I will help take it to them. Funny thing about fighting, *señorita*—men do not want to drink whiskey when they fight or when they are working. They want coffee." She moved aside, and Vicky saw the two largest pots steaming slightly. The cook stood up and paddled the brew with a wooden spoon. "Shall I go for a man to help me with the coffee, *señorita?*" she asked. "Everything is ready. *Si*, it is ready."

Spotted Pony sent scouts to range on either side of his party. He was looking for a specific place he knew to be near. It would be a fine place to set the trap for the eight white eyes that followed.

He began to go over the ground of the spot he had in mind. It was a low growth, not too heavily covered with a thicket. Surrounding the growth like a horseshoe was a slight, sharp rise that was hard to

CALAMITY AT APACHE WELLS 123

see in the dark because of the grass that covered it and the underbrush growth. He would place most of his braves on the rise and in the thickets, and he would stake the woman to the ground as if near an ant hill. Then he would be careful to build a small fire and conceal it just enough to make the scout of the eight believe that he had found the Indian camp.

The thought of soldiers flashed through his mind. Well, he would welcome a fight with the soldiers. He was a bad-hearted Indian whom the whites feared because of his daring raid on the village of Apache Wells and, he said to himself, he was the finest brave that lived. Spotted Pony was the best. None lived that was better.

The white woman did not try to get away. She clung to him tightly and did not complain. Perhaps the white woman pressing against him now wanted Spotted Pony. The thought stirred him deeply.

XVI

Kid Coxe trailed after Austin Bailey and Todd Bain slowly. Their trail was easy to follow. They were heading northwest, and Coxe waited until he was sure of this direction before he made up his mind. It was three o'clock in the afternoon before he came to a section of the land that would tell him for sure where Bailey and Bain were heading. The river was the key. If they crossed the river and headed west, they were going into Mormon country. If they swung north, they would be heading either for Denver or perhaps Wyoming.

It did not bother Kid Coxe that his uncle had tried to kill him. He had been expecting it for some time now, ever since he had started taking over the direction and planning of their movements. Bailey had not said anything openly; neither had Bain, who had been with them longer than Alex Mayer, Curt Hawkins or Grady Potts. But Coxe knew they resented his telling them what to do and were just afraid of his gun enough to keep quiet about it. Only he had not expected them to go against him to his face and give him a chance. For a long while now, every time they bedded down in the open, he had wondered if they would shoot him in the back of his head while he slept.

It was fear, he knew, that made them behave this way. There had been something about fear and the way it acted on the nervous systems of animals. He had read it somewhere in the past—how long ago was it? Several years, John Coxe, since you studied the drawings of the nervous system of a man.

He drifted after Bailey and Bain with the indifference and confidence that had made the others flatter him when he had taken over the planning for the six of them. It had made him smile to himself each time he went to sleep in their company, wondering if tonight they would have enough nerve to pull the trigger—just once—while the six-gun was aimed at the back of his head. He rode in the heat of the afternoon, occasionally reading the trail and the two horse tracks in the dry ground. He did not seem in a hurry to catch up with them and face them down.

It did not occur to Kid Coxe that he might be killed. He did not even think about how he would approach them. He thought back to the morning in the doc's office and the mistake the old man had made in severing the aorta of the young woman, and

Shelby's offer to give him money to go East and study.

He had thought about it before. He did not need Shelby to remind him that a few thousand dollars would put him through medical school. But habit did strange things to men, even young men. He had grown used to the power of his six-gun and the look of fear in other men's eyes when he faced them. He had grown used to living with himself, alone, in the dirty trackless country, roaming from Montana to Mexico, west to California and east to Kansas—he and his stallion that he wished he were riding now. He thought of things that might have been if he had been born with another man and woman for father and mother instead of a drunken coward and a prostitute.

Perhaps, John Coxe thought, as he rode into the range where the river threaded through the rangeland, if he had not had to kill his own father, things might have been different. But who can find a life that means a damn thing and a woman who will give you children, when the look of your son will always remind you that you killed your own fountainhead of life?

He slowed the horse to a walk and studied the trail. Slowly but surely the double track of hoofs was heading north along the river. They were heading for the north. Maybe later they would swing east and head for Denver, but at the moment it looked as though they were taking the route to the north, he bolted the bronc to the east and cut straight across the flatlands. It would mean double riding, covering twice the distance they would cover in half the time, but he felt sure he could do it. He would meet them as they came up the trail where the river turned to the east.

XVII

There were none of Kid Coxe's reflections on life or what might or might not have been in Clint Deane's pursuit of Spotted Pony and his braves. Patrick O'Malley had dropped back to join the others, leaving Deane alone to read the signs in the hard-crusted ground. Why anyone had wanted to settle in the middle of nowhere like Apache Wells escaped him for the moment. Apache Wells was off the beaten path. The trails leading north and south were farther east, and the routes east and west were both north and south. Apache Wells was in the middle of nowhere with little outside interference. Deane knew the answer almost before he asked the question. The springs in and around Apache Wells fed the stream that was never dry. Even with the range burned to a crisp from the six-week drought, the little stream bubbled with fresh water. This was the main reason that the town had been settled and named after the Apache Indians.

CALAMITY AT APACHE WELLS 129

He rode with pleasure, enjoying again and again the energy the black stallion kept reminding its rider that it had. It almost spoke to Deane, and long after they had broken away from the big group that went back to town, the animal was still snorting and chopping the ground with his forefeet, as if impatient to get along.

Clint Deane held the animal in check. O'Malley rode up beside him. "I'm thinkin' that you oughta send out some of us to scout 'round a little bit ahead," he said.

"Jus' thinkin' the same thing myself," Deane answered.

"Want me to go?"

Deane hesitated. He didn't know anything about the brother of the relief stage driver. And he had admitted that Apache Wells was not his town. What would his interest be, with regard to Kathy Roberts? Would he try to kill Indians, or would he consider Kathy Roberts first?

"I think I'll do it. You an' me are the oldest," he said to Patrick O'Malley. "I'll take one of the headstrong young uns an' leave you with the others."

"It was my idea. I'd kinda like to go."

"I got the best horse," Deane said instantly. And there was no contest there. O'Malley's own mount was smaller and much older than the black stallion. "This animal could ride the whole country an' come back an' still beat yours to a frazzle."

Patrick O'Malley frowned, his forehead wrinkled. "That may be, but I know a helluva lot 'bout Indians that you don't know, I'll bet."

"That may be, as you say, but I'm goin' an' you're stayin' with the others," Deane said.

"Tearin' off in this country after Indians like you appear ready to do is the wrong thing, Sheriff," Patrick O'Malley said. "You need me."

"I reckon if I go without you," Deane said, beginning to like the tall brother with the insistent drawl, "you"ll come tearin' after me."

"I might."

"Okay, we'll go together," Deane said. He stopped his stallion and turned to the others. "Me an' O'Malley are goin' ahead to do a little scoutin'. You six men jus' keep comin' in this direction. If anything happens, one of us will get back to let you know 'bout it. If you hear any shootin', come ridin' hellbent fer election."

The six didn't like Deane's decision. They didn't like it at all. But all of them came from Apache Wells and knew that you didn't argue with Clint Deane.

Deane and Patrick O'Malley slapped their mounts lightly, and the two animals jumped out ahead of the others. In a few minutes they were lost in the dust they raised.

It didn't take Clint Deane long to appreciate the

CALAMITY AT APACHE WELLS 131

long-legged and close-mouthed Patrick O'Malley, who rode his bronc as if he were a part of the animal. The man was careful and he was sure. He proved that when they sighted one of Spotted Pony's braves riding loosely up the trail, apparently on the prod at Spotted Pony's rear, checking to see if they were still being followed.

At the same moment O'Malley pointed to a weird-looking collection of weather-blown feathers near a slab of stone. Deane would not have noticed the unusualness of the feathers' position if O'Malley had not pointed it out. Deane was thinking about the Indian brave coming along the trail and was wondering if he should risk a shot or try to take the Indian by surprise. It was then that O'Malley waved Deane's hand back from his six-gun and brought his bronc to a standstill, pointing to the stone just off the trail.

"What is it?" Deane asked.

"Be still, man," O'Malley said.

Deane was not used to being talked to that way. He glared at the lanky puncher and turned to watch the progress of the brave down the trail. "If we stand here, he's gonna see us."

"He won't come any further than that stone," O'Malley said confidently. "Jes' set still, Sheriff."

"How do you know—" Deane asked, and then cut his own question off. He watched as the Indian worked his way closer to them, prodding cautiously, eyes moving. Clint could see the special quality of alertness that all of the Indians had when they were approaching danger, a certain caution in their manner.

The Indian came around the break in the trail, and another few feet would have put him in sight of the two riders. Deane brought out the six-gun but did not fire. O'Malley's hand again waved him down, but Deane was not taking any chances.

Then the most amazing thing happened. The brave stopped a few feet the other side of the stone slab and jerked his pony around as if he had seen a nest of rattlers. Deane heard the Indian's pony retreating before them. He turned to look at Patrick O'Malley, who gave no sign that he thought the behavior unusual. He touched the neck of the bronc with his open hand, and the animal moved ahead.

"What the hell was that all 'bout! That brave skeddaddled like he had seen a ghost," Deane said, moving to O'Malley's side and slipping the six-gun back into his holster.

O'Malley stopped beside the slab of stone. "You might say, in a manner of speaking, he did see a ghost. This is a grave."

"Grave?"

"Indian. And a big shot at that. That's what the feathers mean. Probably some sub-chief. You couldn't have gotten that Indian to pass this stone without puttin' a gun 'gainst his head."

"Well, I'll be damned!" Deane said. He looked sideways at the long face of his companion. "How come you know so much 'bout Indians?"

"I told you that I knew 'em."

"But how?"

"It ain't important, Sheriff," Patrick O'Malley said. "I know 'em—jus' take my word—I know 'em."

"I'll take your word," Deane said. "You damn sure made a believer of me."

"We'll get 'em now. An' there's a chance that we'll get Miss Kathy back, too. That brave will go back an' say there ain't hide or hair of anyone on their trail. Then we'll spook 'em."

"Do what?"

"Spook 'em. Scare the livin' daylights out of 'em."

"How?" Deane asked warily.

"Wait and see, Sheriff. Like I said, I know the Indians. Jus' leave it to me."

"You don't mind if I take my gun, jus' in case?"

"No, I don't mind," O'Malley said in the abrupt, direct way that irritated Deane.

The riders moved on down the trail, moving a little faster now, because it was getting late in the day and they wanted to be as close to Spotted Pony as possible before the sun went down.

XVIII

By four in the afternoon, things in Apache Wells had settled more or less into a pattern. Beds had been brought in for the wounded in the saloon. The wide main street had been cleared, and some of the school children were out raking dust over dried pools of blood. The flap of the wings of the buzzards getting at the horses could be heard all the way into town. And the Indians were buried as they were, the earth dumped in on them without ceremony.

The women had begun to snap out of the first pain and daze of losing their loved ones and were quick with bandages and dressings for those wounded who could be cared for without the assistance of a doctor. Vicky Deane, with the help of Master Shelby, had brought the entire food stock of her kitchen to the center of town on the boardwalk and gave out food to anyone who wanted it.

Coffee cups were near the posts, and all one had to do was dip and drink.

CALAMITY AT APACHE WELLS   135

The shattered glass in the windows of the shop fronts was cleared away, and the jagged edges that had not fallen to the ground were removed. The wagons that had been jerked and torn and turned over were righted, and at a half-dozen places in the street groups of men worked at replacing broken tongues and axles and wheels.

By now the whole town knew of the bank robbery, and though no one spoke of it openly, not daring to say what was in his thoughts, all knew that in addition to the disaster brought on Apache Wells by the Indian raid, there was nothing in the way of help they could look forward to from the bank.

Many of the men who lay dead or wounded had been in town in the hope of getting a loan to keep them going. Now they had even less than when they started. And no one wanted to talk about the attack on the town, or what each secretly hoped Clint Deane would do to the Indians when he caught them. Not one man, woman or child in Apache Wells believed, openly or secretly, that Clint Deane would fail.

Mrs. Grover was the only exception. After seeing that her husband was only superficially wounded, she had turned her energies to helping others. Some of them resented her bossy attitude, but she was a good hand with the sick, and she did something else that no one had thought of. She rounded up a lot of the children who had been all but forgotten, herded them to Vicky's food kitchen and fed them. The widowed and the sorrowful did not restrain themselves and told Mrs. Grover outright to leave them alone, saying they did not want any help from her. But it did not stop her. She went to the side of those who had no one to care for them and with loud cries, sometimes wailing in prayer louder than the sick, tried in her own way to ease their pain and misery.

Paul Roberts had remanied with his father in the livery stable for more than an hour.

Vicky Deane, remembering Kathy, looked up and, turning from her work over the food line, said to Master Shelby standing at her side, "Have you seen that Roberts boy come back yet?"

"No."

"I think you better go down and see about him, Mr. Shelby," she said. "No tellin' what he's liable to do."

Master Shelby nodded and walked toward the livery. He stopped at the huge barn door and moved inside. The room was dark except for a single lantern hanging on a post. The quiet forms beneath the blankets did not bother him. He moved among them and stopped near the light. "Paul Roberts?" he called gently.

Silence.

"Paul!" he called again, this time louder.

CALAMITY AT APACHE WELLS 137

Again there was silence. Shelby was about to turn away and leave when he heard the whimper of a horse in one of the back stalls. He stopped and walked to the rear of the stable quickly. Paul Roberts was in the back, standing with his back to the wall, a saddle blanket in his hand.

"What do you want?" Roberts demanded.

Shelby was so surprised at the boy's manner he did not answer right away. "Just came down to see if you're all right, son," he said finally. "Where are you going? Out to the spread?"

"No."

"That isn't your horse, is it?"

"What difference does it make?" Roberts stepped out of his corner and began adjusting the blanket over the bronc's back.

"Do you have in mind to ride out of town now and go looking for your sister?"

Roberts stopped. "Is that any of your business?"

"In a manner of speaking, it is."

"Well, I don't see how."

"Your brothers and sisters—three of them, anyway —are my pupils. That gives me an interest. What happens to them—" he hesitated— "if you and Kathy and your father are all dead?"

The boy stopped.

"Paul, Clint Deane and more than a half-dozen men who are better prepared than you to find Spotted

Pony are out looking for Kathy. If Kathy is alive—and I'm praying to God that she is—Clint Deane and the others will bring her back. But if you leave now, there's a good chance that you might get killed, and your brothers and sisters will be left without anyone. Would you want that to happen? What would your paw or your maw or even Kathy want you to do?"

"I've got to do something—" the boy protested. "I can't jus' stand 'round, with Paw dead over there—"

Mister Shelby pulled the blanket off the bronc's back and pulled the boy around by the shoulders. "Don't you think you better get back out to your spread and see if everything's all right?"

"But what 'bout Kathy?"

"I'll send word to you the minute I hear," Shelby promised.

"I'll go," Roberts said reluctantly, with a long look at the covered body of his father. "But I ain't gonna tell the young uns 'bout Kathy and Paw. I'll wait a spell, till—maybe Kathy will come back."

"Kathy will be back."

"Yes, sir."

Shelby walked the boy out of the dark livery stable. "What you need is a cup of Miss Vicky's coffee, boy," he said gently.

XIX

Kathy Roberts sat on a blanket and stared into the distance, in the direction from which they had just come, and thought she saw a movement out on the blank, bare horizon, but she was not sure. She had held herself in tightly; but now, in the moment of silence and calm, with the Indians moving off into the growth with the horses and two braves standing guard over her, with the hard ride over and the uncertainty of the future closer than it had been before, she nearly let go. It couldn't have been movement she had seen. It was her eyes, and the heat, and the physical pain of riding for hours on a bareback horse.

She glanced down at her thighs. The insides were red and rough from the animal's hide and the constant rubbing. She did not find herself afraid or humiliated at being naked in front of the Indians. There was little false pride and very little of any pride in Kathy Roberts. If there had been, it would have soon disappeared in her role as mother to her own twin brother and the other children. Countless times since her mother had died, when Saturday night baths were in order, she had stripped down before the family, as they all had done, and bathed with the others. But not since she had become more rounded and mature. Certainly there was girlish modesty in Kathy Roberts, but none of it false. She accepted her nakedness as another unusual aspect of the unusual circumstances of her being there in the first place. She thought about her father and brother and not about being naked before a band of Indians. Her father and brother had been at the wagon when the Indians attacked. What had happened to them?

And the others in town? What had happened to them? Everything had happened so fast. She remembered starting out for Vicky Deane's Lucky-Seven, and that Clint Deane had been walking across the street, and then suddenly, there had been a young boy wearing a gun, and all the people had started coming out of the stores and gathering in the middle of the street. She had known that it was going to be a gun fight and had hesitated, not wanting to see it, hating the idea of having to stand there and watch. She remembered clearly now that she had started across the street the moment she had heard the firing down by the schoolyard. And Clint Deane had yelled something at the young boy and then turned away. And

CALAMITY AT APACHE WELLS

that was when they had come down the street from the school side of town.

She began to shiver, not from the cold, but from a chill in her soul. She could not remember what had happened to her father and her brother, and this worried her more than the fact that she was naked on a blanket while the two Indian guards stared at her body.

It was nearly dark when the trail scout that Spotted Pony had sent back to keep an eye on the eight returned to the growth in the hollow of the horseshoe rise. The Indian slipped his mount, came to the small fire and squatted down. Spotted Pony came over to him.

The scout spoke in a rapid, unfamiliar tongue. Spotted Pony's face was impassive at this news. He knew the omen the brave brought back with him. The day promised to be over in another few minutes. The sun was sinking in the west fast. The omen, Spotted Pony knew, spoke to each of his braves. It was not difficult to see it in all of their faces. He had failed in the hunt for buffalo, then in the raid on the cattle, on the whites and on the stage. True, they had ridden into the white village and killed many, but how many scalps had they taken? There was the promise of more from the eight and the woman before them. But now one of them had seen the eye of the dead. One of their number had seen the place where the spirit re-enters the earth, and they all knew that this would be a bad time for them.

The Indians drifted away from the small fire and returned to their positions on the rise around the hollow and about the growth. Spotted Pony alone remained beside Kathy. He stared at her.

Kathy saw the Indians returning to their positions. She had no way of knowing that they were afraid and that each of them felt the omen the scout had brought back with him was the beginning of their end. She had begun to shiver from the cold as the heat of the day passed, and one of the guards had given her a blanket. She wanted to get closer to the small fire, but she was afraid to move.

Suddenly Spotted Pony began to talk to the others. He started to laugh. He walked around the small fire and talked to the others that she could not see but could hear. Their replies did not indicate they were of the same mind as Spotted Pony.

During the day they had slain a small buffalo calf, and Spotted Pony and the others had gorged themselves. Now Spotted Pony walked around the little clearing, tearing at bloody buffalo meat with strong white teeth and talking to the others. He spoke rapidly and continuously, and then one of the braves came down to the fire and tore at a piece of the meat and talked to Spotted Pony.

The Indian leader threw brush on the fire, and the

CALAMITY AT APACHE WELLS   143

flames leaped high. The flames licked at the darkened sky, and their light cast flickering shadows around the clearing. Another and then another of the braves came to the fire and began to eat, squatting down and listening to Spotted Pony.

The fire was quite large now, and they began to roast the remains of the buffalo calf. They brought piles of dead wood and underbrush, and the calf quarters were soon burned black. The braves would cut a piece of the cooked meat and chew it rapidly, howling when it was too hot and scorched their tongues.

Spotted Pony talked constantly. He laughed, and soon there were a few others who laughed with him. He sat before Kathy, eating a large piece of tender, raw calf meat with a bone through it, tearing off huge chunks which he chewed rapidly and swallowed. He did not give Kathy anything, nor would he allow any of the others, who threw her pieces of the meat as if they were throwing it to a dog, to do so. When this happened the first few times, Spotted Pony snatched it away from her and threw the meat to one side.

The Indians began to look at Kathy as Spotted Pony spoke, and they laughed. One of them came close to her and put his hands on her thighs. Kathy shrank back. The Indian laughed. Spotted Pony spoke again and made repeated gestures toward the braves and then at Kathy. The eating and the gorging on the tender buffalo meat continued until well after dark, and the shadows of the leaping flames, which gave the scene a ghostly, unreal quality, were mingled with the reflections on the naked, sweaty, painted bodies of the braves.

Kathy Roberts knew now what was going to happen. She might have known earlier, deep in her soul, but her courage would not let her think about it. She was confident the town of Apache Wells would not abandon her. But why else would the Indians build such a large fire, and behave in a manner that indicated every confidence in their position?

She knew what was coming, and she shrank away from it. She looked around wildly for a weapon, a knife or a gun, with which she could defend herself, but even as she looked, she knew it would be hopeless to resist. Should she try to fight her way out, she knew the Indians would simply slam her in the head with a rock, or send a quick arrow into her body, and that would be the end of it.

Spotted Pony had finished eating now. He was sitting comparatively quiet, cross-legged, staring at her face, his eyes traveling over her body. He became, with time, almost withdrawn, as if he were thinking about some great problem and had much to think about before he could come to a successful conclusion.

CALAMITY AT APACHE WELLS

The others began to watch him. They too settled down around the fire, cross-legged, and assumed the impassive, unrevealing expressions that Kathy Roberts, a girl raised in Colorado, had seen so often on the faces of the Indians.

She watched Spotted Pony. She stared into his eyes.

Spotted Pony moved toward her slowly, speaking in a chant that might have been a rite of some sort. He did not sound as if he were talking to anyone around him. Soon the others began to chant, picking up and repeating the words that Spotted Pony was saying.

He was a big man, one of the largest Indians Kathy had even seen. He was well over six feet, and his body was smoothly muscled, with no hint of fat or flabbiness.

Kathy shrank back, slipping to the far end of the blanket. Then Spotted Pony leaped forward and picked her up in his arms and carried her around the circle of the others, chanting and listening to the others chant back, and Kathy wondered if she were going to be thrown into the fire as some sacrificial offering.

With slow, deliberate movements, Spotted Pony began walking away from the fire into the darkness. He found a soft spread of buffalo calfskins and put her down. In the distance, a few hundred feet away,

Kathy could see the braves around the fire begin to grin and laugh and cover up their mouths with their hands. A few of them turned and tried to look into the darkness after Kathy Roberts and Spotted Pony.

Kathly came alive. She had not resisted before, but when Spotted Pony began to press her back down onto the spread of calfskins, she began to kick and scratch. She didn't yell—there wasn't anyone to yell to. She tried to get at the Indian's eyes, but he held her wrists. He avoided her kicks and pulled her down to the fur pad.

Kathy began to bite. She sank her teeth into Spotted Pony's arm, but he did not let go. He did not even grunt with pain. She tried again; she kicked desperately with her knees, bringing them up hard, and while Spotted Pony tried to avoid the kick, she managed to get one of his fingers free from her wrist and bit it off.

Spotted Pony released her and screamed with pain. He raised his hand and hit her with his fist. He hit her shoulder and swung again, screaming.

Kathy tried to dodge the blows. The other Indians looked up from the circle of fire and did not grin. They recognized the scream of pain, and they wondered if Spotted Pony was in trouble. They did not question that he would win what he wanted, but it had been a scream of pain.

Spotted Pony hit Kathy again and again, but she

CALAMITY AT APACHE WELLS 147

kept moving around in the darkness, taking the blows on her shoulders and chest. She felt as if her lungs were going to be caved in, but she did not cry out and she did not stop fighting back.

She felt the smeary ooze of Spotted Pony's blood on her body, and then, suddenly, the Indian released her.

She tried to crawl away, and he did not come after her. She looked up, and then Kathy Roberts screamed. She was not sure if she was going out of her mind; she was not sure of anything. She screamed, and then she heard the scream of Spotted Pony behind her, and then the wild curses and yells of the others around the fire. They began to move away. They began to run wildly in the darkness.

Spotted Pony was standing alone, when she turned away from looking at the other thing. She could see him standing against the firelight, his body shining with the flow of blood from his missing finger.

He screamed, and she saw him pull his knife. He lunged beyond her, screaming, yelling, his knife raised in an attack against the thing.

Kathy Roberts closed her eyes. She sat up in the sand and put her hands over her ears and covered her face, bending over her knees, and screaming at the top of her lungs, and then she fainted into unconsciousness.

XX

Kid Coxe had made the long ride up the river and around the bend. He wished over and over that he had that black stallion. His bronc was a fine horse, but it did not compare with the stallion. He kept pressing the animal, thoughtfully studying the land and trying to figure out exactly where Bain and Bailey would leave the river and where he could intersect their trail.

The sun was sinking now. It would be hours before it was dark, but the sun was on its way down. He urged the little horse on and then saw movement ahead. He slowed the horse and came to a dead stop. He studied the movement. It was them all right, and they were moving slowly. Too slowly, he thought.

He cut the bronc hard across the flank, and the pony jumped forward at a dead run. Kid Coxe picked a spot where he wanted to be when they came along, and he had to take the chance of hard riding in the uncertain terrain to make sure that he was at the spot

CALAMITY AT APACHE WELLS 149

in time.

He hung over the horse, riding on his legs, his seat well clear of the saddle, and spoke to the little bronc softly, urging it on. He had no fear of their seeing him. The hard ground would not kick up dust, and the brush was high enough for him to keep well covered. For a full half-hour, Kid Coxe pressed the bronc onward, speaking to it, talking to it. When it faltered, its wind gone, he would slash it angrily on the flank.

He made the spot he wanted, slipped from the saddle and quickly found a place in a nest of rocks for the bronc, hobbling it after a quick search assured him there were no snakes to startle it. He had no fear of the winded little bronc making a noise—unless it was startled or attacked.

Satisfied there were no snakes, he checked his six-gun and made sure that it was free of grit; then he moved to the top of a bald rock and checked Bain's and Bailey's approach.

They were still coming, but more slowly now. Evidently they were satisfied, he thought, that they were not going to be followed.

He saw that Todd Bain rode with one hand on his ear, pressing what looked like a bloody rag to the side of his head. As they drew closer, he could see the two small valises tied together and slung over Austin Bailey's saddle horn. His eyes were a little darker, but not much, and he was not sweating, though he had ridden hard under the late afternoon sun for several hours.

He searched the area for loose rock that might warn them and picked a spot that was well protected.

They came on, both of them quiet, Bain leaning over slightly, holding his ear, and Bailey glancing at him every now and then as if concerned. But Kid Coxe knew that those glances were not caused by concern. He knew, as surely as he knew the sun would set that night, that his uncle was weighing the chances of his calling Todd Bain and outdrawing him. He watched closely. Bain, he saw—and Kid Coxe smiled slightly—was aware of this. Every time Austin Bailey let his pony fall back a few feet, Bain would check his horse and drop back with him. Neither of them made too much of it, but it happened. He waited. He slipped the gun back into the holster and made sure he had good footing. They were only a few hundred feet away now, and it was his plan to stand up and face them. He would give them an even break. After all, Austin Bailey was his uncle.

The two riders came closer to the bald rock.

"Hold on, Austin," Kid Coxe said when the riders drew within range. He stood on the bald rock, his six-gun in the rig, arms dangling at his side.

Austin Bailey and Todd Bain pulled back on the

CALAMITY AT APACHE WELLS   151

reins and stared incredulously at the slim, narrow figure of Kid Coxe. "Kid!" Bailey said.

"I'm callin' you out, both of you," Kid Coxe said.

"Callin' us out—" Bailey glanced at Bain. "But you can't call out your own kin; you can't kill your own uncle."

"I will if I can. An' I'm pretty sure I can. But I'm gonna give you a draw," Kid Coxe said. "You want to try it from your bronc or climb down?"

Bailey jerked his reins. He pointed at Todd Bain. "He was the one that shot at you, Kid. It was Todd. He's always hated you. It was his idea to try an' gun you down—"

Bain sneered. "Cry if you want, Austin; I always knew you didn't have the grit in your gizzard you claimed." He glanced up at Kid Coxe. "You gone an' got yourself into a passel of trouble now, baby boy. I'm gonna leave your guts wide open fer the buzzards to feast on."

"Step down," Kid Coxe said with no emotion at all in his voice.

Bain slipped off the saddle. He stepped away from the horse and dropped his hands.

Kid Coxe watched him. He watched the calm that came over Todd Bain. The man was good. He was just what he was—a killer—and he was going to perform his ritual. He was going to kill. There was no less indifference in Todd Bain's manner than in Kid

Coxe's, but the two men's attitudes were different. Bain wanted to kill, and he wanted to live. Kid Coxe didn't value either killing or living.

Austin Bailey stepped his horse to one side, his eyes on Kid Coxe, wondering if he could draw while the Kid's attention was focused on Todd Bain. But he saw that it was impossible. Kid Coxe was watching both of them.

Bain was out by himself now. He faced the youth on top of the bald rock, and he was ready. He had absolute confidence. He was sure, now that he was faced with a showdown, that he could put Kid Coxe down.

He would use every advantage. He would slip one over on the Kid on top of the rock. He would drop and fade to the left, falling out of the line of fire and getting his six-gun out before he hit the ground. That was important, getting it out and firing before the shock of hitting the ground could jostle his gun hand and throw the shot away. He didn't think, he knew, that there wouldn't be time for a second shot. He would at least have to wound the Kid on the first shot and hope that Kid Coxe would not judge the downward angle of his shot too accurately.

All of this flashed through Bain's mind as he faced the narrow-shouldered youth on top of the rock, a skyline figure that was solid black against the reddening sky.

CALAMITY AT APACHE WELLS 153

There was no thought or conscious decision that this was the moment, or the next moment, or the one after that. There was no count-down, no saying to himself, *I'll draw and move on the count of seven and a half, a nice uneven number of seven and a half;* there was just a muscular reflex action, and the moment had come.

Todd Bain fell to the side as he had planned, but he did not get his six-gun up to fire before he hit the ground. He didn't even get it out of his holster. He died before his hand touched the cold butt.

Kid Coxe watched the round hole trickle blood over Bain's right eye as the man sprawled in the dust. The shot re-echoed through the long afternoon. Then he turned to Austin Bailey.

"Well, Uncle," he said.

"I can't fight my own kin," Austin Bailey said when he had found his voice.

"I don't claim you as kin."

Bailey saw that Bain had done the wrong thing. He had played right into Kid Coxe's hands. He would not draw his gun. He felt sure that Kid Coxe would not shoot him down without a draw. He would outtalk him. He would let Kid Coxe say anything he wanted to, he would let Kid Coxe do anything he wanted to, but he was not going to get Austin Bailey to draw his gun.

Kid Coxe waited. He had slipped the six-gun back

into his holster and stood quietly. He had not even moved the position of his feet. He stood, slightly uneven on the angle of the rock's face, his right knee bent forward a bit, his eyes emotionlessly set on his uncle below, who still refused to get off his horse.

Bailey talked. He begged, he pleaded, he ranted, he raved, he reminded Kid Coxe of how he had taken him in when John had had to run from the law back in Lincoln for killing his own father. He threatened, but he did not make a move for his gun. He kept his hands up high, clearly in view of the young man standing on the bald rock.

"You been talkin' long enough, Austin," Kid Coxe said. "You made up your mind how you want to make your play—on the bronc or down on the ground?"

"I won't draw," Austin Bailey said.

"That your last word?"

"You won't make me draw."

Kid Coxe pulled the six-gun, and it barked once. Austin Bailey was slammed backward out of the saddle and turned a complete flip before he hit the ground flat on his back and sprawled, spread-eagled in the dust, beside Todd Bain, his eyes open, looking as if he had suddenly, mysteriously acquired a third socket that was equally mysteriously empty of an eyeball. He was dead in the split-second it took for the forty-four slug to pass through his brain.

XXI

Clint Deane had been reluctant to go along with the crazy idea of spooking the Indian party when Patrick O'Malley had suggested it, but he had to admit now, seeing the Indians running around in the dark looking for their horses, that he had done the right thing by letting the tall puncher have his way.

The extremely tall, rail-thin body of Patrick O'Malley, naked as the day he was born and covered over with white mud, his head full of feathers, standing on the ground beside his bareback pony that they had also covered with white mud, looked as ghostly as anything Clint Deane could imagine.

It had not taken them long, nor had it been difficult, to trail the Indian scout back to the temporary camp of Spotted Pony. And once they had determined where the Indian leader had gone and seen him return with the buffalo calf, Deane had ridden back to the others and brought them up quickly. But by the time they had returned, Patrick O'Malley was gone, and it was dark.

It had been all Deane could do to keep the others from riding into the camp and blazing away at the Indians. But it had not been too long before half of them were nearly scared out of their wits by Patrick O'Malley appearing suddenly in his birthday suit, painted from head to toe with white mud and wearing head feathers. Some of the boys had wanted to shoot him down right then and there, and would have, with Deane's assistance, if Deane hadn't recognized the extremely long legs of the puncher.

"Man, you shore scared the livin' hell outa me!" one of the others had said when Patrick O'Malley had come into their midst.

"I hope it does the same thing fer that bunch of savages," O'Malley replied. "As soon as they start messin' 'round with Miss Kathy yonder," he added, "several of you boys go out an' take a position between the Indians an' their mounts. The rest of you get 'round in back of me, 'cause some of them may not be fooled an' try to slam a hatchet in my gizzard."

It had been difficult for them to watch the Indian pick Kathy up and walk with her around the fire, exhibiting her to the others. They were brave strong men, and they respected womanhood more than they

CALAMITY AT APACHE WELLS 157

respected honor and truth, if the woman was a good woman.

But they listened to Patrick O'Malley, and they did what he told them to do. Clint Deane, seeing Spotted Pony rush the skinny figure of Patrick O'Malley, brought up his six-gun and fired, but Spotted Pony continued to come on. He did not even falter. Deane wondered if he had missed. The others began to fire, and Deane saw the Indian take a headlong dive in one last attempt to get to the white, ghostly figure of Patrick O'Malley.

Deane's group rushed the fire then, hearing the guns of the others on the other side of the fire open up and hearing the screams of the Indians as they tried to get to their mounts.

It was as brutal as it was simple. The Indians were caught unarmed, frightened by the spirit figure of Patrick O'Malley and penned between the accurate, rapid fire of the citizens of Apache Wells.

It was over in less than a minute, once the firing began. Each man emptied his six-gun, and each man was satisfied when it was over. Every Indian brave in the group was dead.

They picked up Kathy Roberts, wrapped her carefully in a blanket and climbed back to their horses. They left the fire burning; they left the bodies of the Indians where they fell. They did not take any of the guns or knives or any of the possessions of the Indians. They did not even take the horses. They had come to kill and pay revenge, and they had.

They had not planned it that way, but it worked out that Apache Wells was still wide awake, and the lights in the saloon, in the Lucky-Seven and several other places along the main street, were burning brightly when the band returned with Kathy Roberts.

"Paul! Paul!" Vicky Deane shouted to the young man, who had not moved from the chair near where the Mexican cook had set up the food kitchen. "They've come back, and Kathy is all right."

Paul Roberts looked up. He got slowly to his feet, as if in a trance, and walked to greet Clint Deane, who carried Kathy Roberts in his arms.

A group had arrived from Shiprock, and the health and the warmth and the willing spirit of the Shiprock people spread through Apache Wells like a soothing balm. They came into the saloon, gently pushed the tired women to one side and took over the care of the sick and wounded. They got the children rounded up, and a half-dozen Shiprock mothers began bedding them down in the hotel, three and four in a bed. Some went to the Lucky-Seven and relieved the Mexican cook and began cleaning up, while others took over the shops and stores, taking down things that were needed and carefully marking down every item in the book.

CALAMITY AT APACHE WELLS 159

The men, too, began at once to plan how they could repair the broken fronts of the few houses that had been torn down by the stampeding wagon teams when the Indians had circled back and forth in the main street.

But there was no doctor. And however much they could do for the people of Apache Wells, the helpful, ready people of Shiprock could not prevent one of the local boys from dying, and the good spirits they had brought with them were visibly affected when several of the men carried the fifteen-year-old boy down to the livery stable.

Then someone remembered the half-breed, Big Foot. The half-breed's name was on everybody's lips, and the men stopping for a quick cup of coffee all agreed that if anyone could get to Tipp City and bring back a doctor, Big Foot could do the job.

"There ain't a better man fer the job in the whole state of Colorado."

"An' by God, he'll run that mouse-colored bronc to the ground an' then—"

"Then he'll git off an' run hisself down to a nub, but that half-breed Injun will fetch a doctor."

"He won't let Apache Wells down."

The tall brother of Foster O'Malley was passing the coffeepot at the time. He had known Big Foot for years as a close friend. The old Indian half-breed had taught him and his brother every Indian trick and all the lore he knew.

He had helped them live. And he remembered bitterly the time Big Foot had come to Foster and him, and told them the people of Apache Wells had threatened Vickers' life if he lent money to Big Foot for the spread the man had wanted to buy so badly.

He did not stop as he heard the men's comments. Patrick O'Malley did not look at them. He spat at their feet, kept his head down and his right hand near the handle of his six-gun and said one word: "Hypocrites!" Then he ambled on in his lanky meaningful fashion, still smeared with the white mud in which he had faced forty savage and frightened Indians who had rushed to their deaths.

One of the younger men bristled. "Now what did he mean by that!"

Clint Deane heard it and, with several of the older heads in the group, held the boy in check. They did not explain. They were too ashamed.

Deane moved through the dark town restlessly, his head and eyes moving as if looking for someone. He was so absorbed in his search that he did not see Vicky Deane come to the door of the Lucky-Seven and start to speak. He walked on, up and down the alleys, and finally went down to the livery stable and, with a tight jawline, looked under each of the blankets.

Master Shelby and Douglas Vickers found him as

he was leaving the stable. "Who're you lookin' for, Clint?" Douglas Vickers asked.

"A feller."

"Who?" Shelby asked, puzzled.

"Young feller that helped Doc out with the doctorin' this mornin' when the stage came in," Deane said. "He might be able to do somethin' fer those people inside the saloon."

Vickers and Shelby looked at each other. "You know about the bank, don't you, Clint?" Vickers asked.

"The bank?" Deane's eyes were slitted.

"It was robbed," Shelby said, "right after the attack."

Clint Deane cursed. He turned around and started for the middle of the town and the knot of men around the saloon.

XXII

Kid Coxe had not moved after taking the two small valises from the saddle horn of the horse. He released the cinch straps from the two horses, removed the bits and bridles and set the horses free.

He sat down on the nearest saddle and opened the valises. The money was in thick packets, and there was exactly seventy-seven thousand dollars. He closed the tops of the valises and rolled a cigarette. He glanced at the body of Todd Bain and then over at Austin Bailey and did not look at them again. He was alone.

He smoked thoughtfully, staring up at the sky and wondering about things that had bothered him since he was a boy, since he had killed his father and had had to go on, making his way with the gun, continuing to kill. He saw that killing his father had altered his life as surely as if someone had caught him and branded him with a hot iron and then penned him inside an inescapable place and owned

CALAMITY AT APACHE WELLS

him. What other thing could he have done?

Austin Bailey had done for him what he was capable of doing. It was again the thing, that irreconcilable thing that had brought him to the little shadow below the bald rock, death in the air, death that he had caused himself. If he had not killed his father he would not have had to live with Austin Bailey, who was, by trade and occupation and intent, a thief and a murderer. Bailey had taught him how to do what he had known how to do: rob a bank, rustle cattle, bushwhack a stage or a rider; how to draw a six-gun, how to shoot a carbine, how to live. It was not John Coxe's fault that the way Austin Bailey had lived had been outside the law, or that he had taught John Coxe to live by the code that he, Austin Bailey, lived by.

It had started when John had killed his father, and had started to live with Austin Bailey. The education he had received in how to be a gunfighter and a killer and a thief had brought him now to the place where he had killed his kin again.

And if he had not killed his father, Kid Coxe thought he would have gone to live with an aunt in Chicago. He had planned to run away from home as soon as he finished that year in school. And the aunt in Chicago would have helped him to go to a good school, because she was well off and owned her own house and ran her own business. Then he would have been a doctor, a man who saved lives instead of destroying them.

He looked at the money. It was more than enough for him to leave Colorado and go to some Eastern city and finish his education, and then go on to medical school and become a doctor. But how long would it take? Five years? No, longer. Ten at the very least, even if he did nothing but study.

Ten years. He would be about thirty then. He could be a cultured man and could hope to marry a cultured, refined woman and have a home. There was no one to stop him. The money was there. He could take this way out and leave the past behind him. No more killing. He would escape the pen and remove the brand of killer, gunfighter, thief from his name.

He did not move, even when it grew dark and there wasn't anything in the darkness but the red glow of his cigarette as he sat on the saddle and occasionally slapped at a gnat. Even when he heard the scrape of a coyote in the brush, scenting out the death scene, and heard the thrash of buzzards' wings overhead, he did not move.

Kid Coxe rode out with slow patience. The pony was not strong, and the only regret he had was that he was not forking the big stallion. He let the small bronc pick its own trail through the rocky spots, dropping into ravines and plodding along on the sandy bottoms, his thoughts in the future. Well, here was the time, he thought, with the money and a clear shot for whatever might be ahead. He wondered now, riding the barren stretches of Colorado, if he would learn to be a doctor. He thought about the foreign languages necessary before one could begin medical school. He shrugged his shoulders. "If others can learn to speak them, by God, so can I," he said aloud, and his voice sounded strange in his ears.

There was a sudden rattle of a snake. The little pony skittered to the side of the trail to get away from the crawling menace, backing up and throwing Kid Coxe to the ground. The animal bolted a dozen yards and then suddenly went down to the ground with a heavy thud and crash. Even from where he sprawled in the grass, Kid Coxe heard the animal's leg bone snap where the frightened bronc had stepped in a gopher hole.

Kid Coxe got up and dusted himself off. He listened and heard the burr of the snake again. Cautiously he sought it out and, with a single shot from the six-gun, separated the snake from its head. He then turned his attention to the little bronc. He felt the leg and knew even before he touched the break that it was useless. He stepped back and put a bullet into the bronc's brain. The shot echoed and died out in the wide range country. Kid Coxe took the money and the canteen from the saddle, pulled his carbine out of the boot and turned toward the Apache Wells-Tipp City road. It would be useless, he knew, to try to go back for Bailey or Bain's horse. His best chance would be to get over on the road and take the mount of the next rider that came along.

He began walking quickly now, because he wanted to get out of that part of the country now that he had made his decision.

It did not take him too long to find the trail that would lead down to the road, and then he began legging it hard. The going was rough in high-heeled boots, but he had perseverance.

He walked for hours without stopping. And it was gray dawn before he hit the main road. He walked north toward Tipp City and away from Apache Wells for a mile or so, found a good place between two rocks that were in the middle of a long straight stretch. He took a drink of water from the canteen and began to wait. It was full blue dawn by the time he had settled in and smoked a cigarette. The sun had not broken the horizon and wouldn't for another hour, but it was light.

Another drink of water, and then he heard it. He listened. A steady unbroken patter, heavy and fast. Someone was riding hard, that was for sure. He set himself and waited.

The rider came down the road at a long flat run,

his hat brim buckled against the press of the wind. Kid Coxe waited until the man in the saddle would find it impossible to draw a gun and defend himself; and if he refused to stop and rushed past, Kid Coxe could wing him. He stepped out into the road, fired once in the air and leveled the carbine at the oncoming rider.

"Sorry, mistuh," he said gently, "but I need your horse." He pointed the carbine at the big roan bronc.

XXIII

Clint Deane listened to the accounts of the bank robbery from Master Shelby and the others who had seen a little of it and heard the shooting, his face lined as he removed his six-gun from the rig and examined it. "Three of 'em, huh?" He pulled out the circulars that he had shoved into his pocket, remembering them suddenly as if they were another part of another life, at least ten years ago. He held out the pictures of Austin Bailey and Todd Bain. "Is this anything like 'em?"

Master Shelby clenched his teeth and shook his head. "I didn't get a close look at them myself."

"Yeah," a man said. And then several more agreed. "That's them," was the general chant. "And there was one more. That little feller that helped the doc with the woman when the stage come in," an old man added.

"The one," Paul Roberts said, "that you were bracing in the middle of the street when the Injuns

CALAMITY AT APACHE WELLS 169

hit."

"Kid Coxe," Deane said. "When did they leave?" He was busy transferring shells from Douglas Vickers' belt to his own.

"Right after the fight, an' a little after you left town with the others, but 'fore Vickers an' the others come back. They headed north. Ain't been nobody come in from Tipp City, so we don't know if they went straight north or veered to the northwest or the northeast," a raw-boned puncher said.

Deane considered this. It was a good chance. "Find me a fresh horse, if that's possible," he said to a man. "You want to come along, O'Malley?"

'You goin' after them tonight?" Shelby asked.

"Any reason why not? They might think we're gonna take it easy after bein' hit so hard by the Indians, an' jus' lope along. If they do, I'll get 'em."

"And do what?" Shelby asked.

"What's that supposed to mean?" Deane asked.

"I mean—" Shelby stopped. His eyes had settled on Vicky Deane pushing her way into the group. He looked at her hard, but she did not see him. She was looking at Clint Deane. She did not even look in Master Shelby's direction. She pushed through the men and came to his side. She put one hand on his arm.

"Well, what is it, Schoolteacher?" Deane asked.

Shelby's face tightened.

Deane continued inserting shells into the web of his belt and did not look up. Shelby looked at Vicky. "Kid Coxe is a friend, and he did not rob the bank," Shelby said.

The men in the group murmured, and Deane looked up slowly. "A friend? You have strange friends, Schoolteacher."

"John Coxe was a pupil in my last teaching post back in Lincoln—"

"Come on, O'Malley," Deane said, turning away from Shelby.

"Listen to me, Clint. Coxe will be back. He tried to stop them from robbing the bank."

"I got a circular in my pocket fer that man," Deane said, stopping long enough to finish his sentence, "an' I might as well tell you right now that I ain't got much use fer a man that will ride in when a town is being raided by Indians an' rob the bank."

"What happens if you meet him on the trail coming back with money?" Shelby asked.

"If I find him with the money—" He stopped. "No, Schoolteacher, let's put it this way. If I find your friend Coxe, and I will, I'll bring him in."

Vicky Deane let out a gasp. "Clint, no—"

The townspeople of Apache Wells and Shiprock pressed in close to watch the sudden conflict between the two best-liked men in Apache Wells. And there wasn't one of them that didn't know they were rivals

CALAMITY AT APACHE WELLS 171

suing for Vicky Deane's hand in marriage.

"What is it, Miss Vicky?" Deane asked.

Vicky Deane was silent.

"He'll kill you, Clint, if you go up against him with a gun," Shelby said. "I've seen him. I've seen him draw, man; he'll gun you before you can clear leather."

Something snapped inside Clint Deane. He twisted around and grabbed Master Shelby by the gun belt and jerked him out into the street. He had his six-gun out and rammed into Shelby's stomach. And then both men froze hard, because Master Shelby had his gun cocked and rammed into Deane's stomach.

They stood toe to toe, fingers stiff on the triggers of their guns, their eyes searching each other's.

"He matched Clint Deane's draw!" someone exclaimed.

"Gawddamn, I seen everything now," another voice said.

The street was cold and silent. There wasn't one who watched that didn't know this was death. After the surprise of Master Shelby's draw on even terms with Deane's had worn off, they turned their eyes to watch Vicky Deane. The pretty young widow hesitated. She knew that the slightest move by either man would mean a double death. A nervous twitch of either man's finger, and both guns would go off.

There was no escape. They had to back off. The town of Apache Wells knew this. And Clint Deane and Master Shelby knew it, too.

Which one would crawl?

"I'm the law, Schoolteacher. I got my job to do," Deane said, his lips hardly moving.

"And I'm the schoolteacher, lawman, and I got my job to do," Shelby answered.

"Your friend is wanted."

"That may be, but I'm going to see that he gets a chance to prove himself one way or the other," Shelby replied.

"He broke the law."

"Not in Apache Wells; in this town he didn't," Shelby said.

They had not moved. There was no more than ten inches between their faces. When they spoke, their voices were low and hardly audible to those standing on the boardwalk.

"They gonna stand there all night?" someone asked.

"You figure on stoppin' 'em?" a voice replied.

"Miss Vicky can stop her man," Mrs. Grover said.

The crowd murmured. Sure, Miss Vicky could prevail. But which one would she go to? And was there any guarantee that the man who lost out wouldn't fire anyway?

CALAMITY AT APACHE WELLS 173

"I—I—please—" Vicky Deane pleaded.

Neither man moved. "I'm going to count to three," Douglas Vickers said, pushing his way through to the front. "I want both of you to step back and lower your guns."

Neither Shelby nor Deane appeared to hear the banker.

"Listen to me, Clint, Shelby!" Vickers pleaded. "Both of you know that you can't win—step back."

"Stay out of this, Douglas," Deane said.

Shelby remained silent.

"I'm gonna count to three," Deane said to Shelby, "and then I'm gonna cut you down, Schoolteacher."

Shelby was silent.

"One—"

Shelby's jawline tightened. "I'll back away, if you'll give Kid Coxe until full sunup to come back. And if he ain't back by then, I'll go with you to hunt him down."

"Two—"

"You do your job protecting this town, and I do my job protecting minds and teaching young uns and helping them to get on the right track. If you can't see that, then you better say three. You didn't have anybody messing you up when you went after the Indians and brought Miss Kathy back. You saved Miss Kathy—and I'm trying to save John Coxe. Tell me there's a difference, lawman."

"Miss Vicky, she's fainted!" someone yelled. The crowd pressed in tightly around the fainting woman. No one noticed or heard Clint Deane finish his count.

"Three!"

Shelby backed away and dropped his gun hand to his side. He did not take his eyes away from Deane's face. "You know I'm right, Clint."

Deane slipped his gun into the rig. "You have until first sun; then I'm ridin' out to get him."

"I'll ride with you," Shelby said, and slipped his gun into his holster, turned and walked into the saloon.

Deane strode down the street toward the sheriff's office.

It was getting cold, the way it does before the sun rises, and the eastern edges of the country were not so gray as they had been before, but more blue now. They took Vicky Deane into the hotel, and several of the women brought her out of the faint easily.

"What—what happened to—"

"To whom, honey?" Mrs. Grover asked. "Which one you worried about?"

Vicky turned to another woman. "They're both all right," the woman replied. "They're going to wait until first sun for the Coxe boy to come back."

"And then?" Vicky Deane asked, holding back the fear, the dread she had felt, remembering the fluid motion, the absolute flawless effort coupled with

CALAMITY AT APACHE WELLS 175

blurred speed when Kid Coxe had drawn his gun in the Lucky-Seven Restaurant.

"Then, honey," Mrs. Grover said sincerely, "they're both going to ride out and hunt him down like a mangy dog."

XXIV

The town of Apache Wells waited for two things that would mean life or death. They waited for the doctor to help with the wounded in the saloon. And they waited for Kid Coxe to come back with the money and preserve the life of their town.

They waited in tight, tension-filled groups along the town's main street. These were the cattlemen who knew that a broken bank would break their lives. They stood on one booted heel and then the other. They moved restlessly, and their eyes never stopped searching for signs of dust, a telltale warning of Kid Coxe's return. These were hard-handed, hard-eyed men who had their lives in the countryside around Apache Wells. They told stories, quiet tales of courage and bravery; stories that were unspoken but communicated in the quickness of a hand to the mouth to remove a cigarette, in a gesture to hitch up trousers or to turn suddenly at a sound, in eyes alert to find the source and see. Money had never

CALAMITY AT APACHE WELLS

meant very much before. They hadn't come there from Kansas and Nebraska to make money. They had come to create a home. And money had never been important before. But now it was. Now all of a sudden, the fifteen or twenty or thirty years they had put into making this land provide for them and their families hinged on money. It made the cattlemen edgy, and there were a few fights, some of them mean. But when the explosive tempers were cooled, there wasn't any deep anger. They washed off at the spring and continued to wait.

It was not quite the same for those in the saloon, those with wounds who might die if the doctor didn't come. Here, too, there was an eye to the road and an ear for the pounding of hoofs. They waited for the man from Tipp City. The women, too, showed their tempers. They flared at the children. They grew bitter. They remembered too much of their lives that had gone into supporting their men and the loss they had taken when the drought had hit.

They waited for the doctor to arrive from Tipp City, and they were not unmindful of their men waiting for the boy to come back with the money.

Some of the men in the hotel lobby started a poker game for pennies. But Mrs. Grover put a stop to this. She busted up the game and told them off roughly, waving her Bible, and before anyone knew it, they were singing hymns and were dropping to their knees to pray. Some others thought it would be better to go down to the church, and they did. But the singing and the prayer meeting did not have much spunk to it. They sang raggedly, and if the slightest noise could be heard outside, they would stop and turn to listen, sharply, to see if one of them might be the boy or the doctor.

The gray dawn gave over to full blue, and it would be sunup in less than an hour. The prayer meeting broke up. The men at the spring began to rouse themselves, and some of them began to walk toward the end of town to get a better view of the trail. The women moved to the door of the saloon, and the boardwalk in front of the hotel was full. They talked little now. Their eyes burning from the day, the raid, the hard riding, the night of little or no sleep, they stood and waited.

The talk of the town at first was about which one Vicky Deane would pick: Master Shelby or Clint Deane? Deane had only proved once more, with steely determination, what the town already knew: that he was a tough fighter and still doing his job. "Look," they said, "at the way he got Kathy Roberts back and paid off them Indians."

But there was another group that looked beyond the immediate drama and emotions of the twenty-four hours of conflict in the small cattle town. It was fine to have a good upstanding schoolteacher like

CALAMITY AT APACHE WELLS 179

Master Shelby to teach the young uns, and it was good to see a man stand toe to toe with Clint Deane. But what, just what, if that Kid Coxe didn't come back, with the money? What then? It would mean a couple of hours start and the chances of the trail cooling off.

And who had prevented Clint Deane from hitting the trail hard and fast after the money and the bandits? Master Shelby.

This group that looked ahead to the continuing drought-ridden country, a country that was nearly parched, was loud and voiced its opinions openly and more boldly as the blue dawn began to fill the eastern sky.

Deane heard it. Shelby heard it. And Vicky Deane heard it. But no one made a direct accusation. Not against Deane, for backing down and giving in to Shelby's demand to wait and see if Kid Coxe would show up. And not against Shelby for defending his friendship with Coxe. And wasn't there a little talk about someone remembering seeing the Coxe boy six-gunning it out with Austin Bailey and Todd Bain at the bank?

The groups along the main street watched closely as Clint Deane came out of his office and began saddling the big stallion. Shelby came out of the saloon and blinked in the bright blue light and nodded to Patrick O'Malley standing at the hitch rail. Both men began saddling their broncs. When they were finished, they stood to one side and waited. The whole town squinted from one end of the street to the other for some sign of the Coxe boy or the doctor. They did not talk much. Someone had gone down to the Lucky-Seven and brought back a big pot of coffee, and they had cups of it, black and without sugar, and did not take their eyes off the street.

The sun was not up yet, but Deane threw a leg over the saddle and settled into the stirrup. He walked the stallion slowly down to the saloon and waited.

"Where you think they went, O'Malley?" he asked again, remembering that O'Malley had suggested the northeast and a run for Denver.

But O'Malley didn't answer. Deane and Shelby avoided each other's eyes. But Vickers came out of the saloon with a gun rig strapped around his middle, carrying a carbine. He began saddling up. No one spoke a word. Gradually the little groups began to move down to the front of the saloon and stood around, waiting to overhear something, waiting for the sun—waiting for Kid Coxe.

It wouldn't be long now. Another fifteen or twenty minutes, and the sun would break the eastern rim. O'Malley collected the canteens and walked to the bubbling spring and filled all four of them and went back, giving a full canteen to the other three men. He sat down and began cleaning his carbine, working

CALAMITY AT APACHE WELLS 181

quickly, deftly, not really watching what his hands were doing but working from feel and keeping his eyes flicking from one end of the street to the other.

"About ten minutes, I'd say," Douglas Vickers said, standing in his stirrups to stare into the east. "Don't you think we'd better ride?"

No one answered him. And no one made a move to wheel his bronc. They waited, with the cold morning silence hanging around them like the dew that had settled the dust in the street.

Vicky Deane stood in the lobby of the hotel and watched the men, who in turn were keeping their eyes on the sun ridge to the east.

There was not much time. They would be riding out soon, and they would not be facing a group of savages. They would be up against a deadly gunfighter—a killer. Vicky Deane could not forget the eyes in the restaurant and the way they had looked at her.

The minutes were ticking past. O'Malley had moved to his horse and pulled up into the saddle. Only Master Shelby remained on the ground now, leaning casually over the rail, holding the reins of his bronc in his hands, staring at his hands, now and then glacing up to stare down the street.

There always had been but one man for her, from the time her husband had died. From the first time he had walked into her life, she had known that she would marry him. She had never seriously considered the other man.

How much alike they are, she though suddenly, as if seeing it for the first time. Both of them are strong and wise, each in his own endeavor. Both of them are considerate and gentle, and both of them are in love with me. And yet the chemicals of one were the exact mixture, the precise formula for her, and the other was all wrong. Like black and white, she thought, staring at both of them.

Not much time left now, she knew. She would have to go out and speak to him. Just a few more minutes. She would have those minutes, she thought, determined. She would call him to one side and bring him into the dark lobby of the hotel and say the things she had wanted to say for so long.

She opened the door. The noise broke the silence of the street, and the four men who were ready to ride out turned to look at her. Then the people who were standing around turned to look also.

Master Shelby straightened up, and Clint Deane raised himself in his stirrups, tipping his hat.

"Good mornin', Miss Vicky," someone said as she stepped through the door. "Hope you're feeling better."

Vicky Deane nodded and smiled. She stepped to the edge of the boardwalk and looked down at the group forty feet away. Shelby and Deane were within

CALAMITY AT APACHE WELLS 183

six feet of each other.

She opened her mouth to call him.

"Here he comes!" someone shouted.

Vicky Deane turned like a shot and stared down the main street. She saw a roan with a big chest and two men riding.

"He's come back!" a shrill-voiced puncher yelled. "An' he brought the doctor with him!"

The two men rode the tired and staggering roan to the rail.

"Where are the sick people?" the doctor demanded. He pulled his bag from the saddle and slipped to the ground. "Somebody take care of my horse and get me a quart of liquor. See you later, John."

"Yes, Doc," Kid Coxe said, a weary smile on his face. He turned to Master Shelby. "There's your doctor, and here's the town's money, Mistuh Shelby."

Clint Deane started to turn the big stallion away and ride from among the yelling, whooping crowd, but Kid Coxe's voice stopped him. "You're ridin' my bronc, lawman," he said.

Deane stopped. He hesitated. "Yes, I guess I am." He slipped out of the saddle and tied the stallion to the hitch rail, then turned and walked silently and alone down the side of the boardwalk.

XXV

"I'll be movin' on, Mistuh Shelby," Kid Coxe said. He walked with the schoolteacher to the big stallion and held the reins a moment, staring at the back of Clint Deane as the big sheriff walked toward the office, then disappeared inside. "Why didn't he brace me? I can't figure it out."

"He's a fair man, John," Shelby said. And then he told the young man of the decision to wait until sunup before going after him. John Coxe listened, unable to bring his eyes up to the level of his friend's. "We were ready to ride out when you came in."

"Were you gonna ride with 'em?" Coxe asked.

Shelby nodded.

"Then I'm glad I came back," Coxe said. He swung into the saddle. "I wasn't plannin' to. I might as well tell you that now." He explained how he had caught and killed Austin Bailey and Todd Bain. "I was gonna follow your advice an' take the money, go

East an' finish my education, then go to medical school. Then I met the doc from Tipp City. He told me how an Indian half-breed had run halfway across the state to search him out and that he was on the way to help you people. I saw it then. Even if I became a doctor, it wouldn't be right. I wouldn't ever be able to do enough for people to make up for the wrong I would be doin' by takin' the doc's horse an' lettin' the people inside the saloon maybe die. Not countin' what would happen to the people that would be just as bad off with the town sucked dry of its money."

"What are you going to do now?" Shelby asked. "Stay, John. Stay here in Apache Wells, finish your education with me and then go East. You've made friends here; we'll help you."

"No, Mistuh Shelby. I had my chance to be a doctor out there on the Tipp City road, an' passed it by. I already done more fer a whole townful of people by bringin' them their doctor and returnin' their money than I would ever be able to do as a doctor myself."

"Have you any plans?"

"I figure I might go on to California," John Coxe said. "Somethin' new an' different. Not many people have heard of me out there."

"Good luck, John. I'll never forget you."

"I don't reckon I'll ever forget you, Mistuh Shelby. You teach your young uns good now, you hear?"

He smiled, nodded his head and touched the stallion's sides with his heels. The animal drifted out to the middle of the street and headed west and away from the rising sun. There weren't many people left outside the saloon to watch him leave. Most of them had gone with Douglas Vickers to the bank to count the money, and others had gone into the saloon to watch the doc from Tipp City take care of the wounded. But the few that watched John Coxe ride out of Apache Wells knew that their lives would never be so close to destruction as they had been when the young gunfighter had decided to return to Apache Wells with the bank's money and the Tipp City doctor. A few of them waved slightly, lifting their hands in a half-hearted gesture, almost ashamed. But Coxe did not look at them. He kept his head and eyes straight ahead and rode out of sight around the edge of the last building and was gone.

It was seven o'clock, and the sun was fully up when the doctor wiped his hands and stepped out onto the boardwalk. "That's the last of them," he said to Shelby wearily.

"They'll live?" Shelby asked.

"Every one of them," the doctor replied. A woman approached the doctor and thanked him for saving her baby. "Yes, ma'am," the doctor replied. "This

CALAMITY AT APACHE WELLS   187

town sure took a beating," he said to Master Shelby.

"Yes. But it'll be a better town for it."

"What do you mean?"

"Nothing like a good fight to pull a town together and get them to work together. Every man in the country has cattle that needs to be driven up to winter grass, but some of them have been holding out. I think they'll make the drive now."

"By Shaw! Guess I'll go get a little shut-eye. Going to have a rough day, with a couple of them inside." He walked away toward the hotel lobby just as the children that had been bedded down by the Shiprock mothers came out, bright-eyed, faces scrubbed clean and alive.

"Any school today, Mistuh Shelby?" they asked, and gathered around the schoolteacher.

"There sure will be, and don't be late," he said.

Now he had to get a little shut-eye. He would have a hell of a day in the school shed. It was going to be difficult to keep them away from thoughts of the raid and the deaths and the robbery. It was going to be a hell of a day. But first he would get a cup of coffee at the Lucky-Seven.

Vicky Deane worked with the Mexican cook to get the grits and the bacon and the pancake batter ready. The restaurant was full. Douglas Vickers had counted the money and told everyone that there wasn't so much as a thin dime missing. Vicky brought the platter of eggs, bacon and grits out to the banker and turned to look at the happy eager faces of the cattlemen.

"Think we ought to whip up a special meeting, Mistuh Vickers, and set 'bout plannin' fer a drive to the winter grass?" Paul Roberts asked.

"That's the only way you're going to save yourselves." Vickers replied.

The men began to talk, agreeing that there was no real objection to driving the combined herds to the north. Old friends seemed to be closer than before as they hunched over their breakfasts, and old enemies had forgotten their reasons for disliking each other.

Shelby came into the Lucky-Seven and sat down in his usual place. "Good morning, Miss Vicky," he said.

Vicky Deane smiled warmly. "Good morning, Master Shelby," she said. "The usual?"

"Please, ma'am."

Shelby sat beside the window and studied the street. The wagons began moving in and out now. There were several in front of the general store. The Roberts kids were a little subdued over the death of their father, but Shelby knew children and knew they would bounce back soon enough. Kathy Roberts was hovering around them, a little pale and with dark circles under her eyes, but still pretty. Mrs. Grover

CALAMITY AT APACHE WELLS 189

was talking loudly to a group of the Shiprock people who were preparing to leave and return to their homes, and the loafers in town were near the spring, some of them already asleep in the shade. There wasn't too much difference, Shelby thought, except that there were a few familiar faces missing.

Vicky Deane brought him his breakfast. "Thank you," Shelby said, and then suddenly he turned to her. "Miss Vicky, I've been meaning to speak to you—"

Vicky blushed. "What on earth about, Master Shelby?"

The dining room quieted and listened. But Shelby didn't continue. Clint Deane's heavy step sounded on the boardwalk, and the sheriff opened the door and entered. He grinned. "Mornin'." And then, with a cheery wave at Shelby and Vicky, he took his usual place.

Vicky turned a deep crimson. The others in the room began to cough, and Douglas Vickers got up, though he had not half finished his breakfast, and jerked his head for the others to follow. In a moment the room was empty except for Master Shelby and Clint Deane.

That was the way it was when Vicky returned with Clint Deane's breakfast. She placed it before the sheriff and then backed off. Her face was still flushed. Out of the corner of her eye she saw Douglas Vickers and the others peeking in through the window.

"Nice morning," she said.

Neither man replied, but each grunted and turned to his food.

"Would you like some more coffee, Clint?

"No, thank you."

"Would you like some, Mister Shelby?"

"No, thank you, Miss Vicky."

"Well, I'll just have a cup myself." She turned to the kitchen.

"Miss Vicky!" Shelby called sharply, and stood up. He glanced at Clint Deane. The sheriff kept his head down, shoveling in his food without tasting it. "I don't see why this should continue any longer, Miss Vicky."

"What on earth do you mean, Master Shelby?"

"Me and Clint and you," he said.

"Why, I never heard such a bold thing in my life—" She gasped.

"Clint loves you, Miss Vicky."

Clint Deane gagged on his food. He spun around. "I guess I can do my own declarin', Schoolteacher!" he snapped.

"Sure you can, you big baboon," Shelby said, smiling easily. "Why don't you?"

Clint and Vicky looked at each other and then at Shelby. "I —well, I don't know."

"You don't have any competition, Clint. I'm de-

CALAMITY AT APACHE WELLS 191

claring out right now," Shelby said, still smiling. "Beside, I've known all along that Miss Vicky loved you."

"You what!"

Shelby nodded. "Vicky told Kathy, and Kathy told me."

"Kathy," Shelby said. He grinned broadly. "It's always been Kathy Roberts."

"But—but—" Deane stammered. "I thought that it was—"

"Miss Vicky?" Shelby walked over and took her hand. "At first I thought it was Miss Vicky. But when the Indians took Kathy—I knew then—"

He walked to the door and stepped out, holding the door open and talking back inside, loudly enough for everyone to hear. "Maybe we can make it a double wedding," Shelby said.

The stores were opened and the schoolbell rang as usual, and the cattlemen lined up outside the railing in Vickers' bank and got their loans. All of the wounded in the saloon would live. The sky was bright blue, and there was no hint of rain in the sky. The meeting of the cattlemen was arranged for that night to plan the drive of the combined herds to Wyoming for winter grass.

And the men in the shade of the big tree near the spring talked and retold over and over the tale of the strange day; a day when a young gunman had become a doctor; when nearly fifty Indians were scared out of their wits by a skinny puncher; when a bank robbery had been executed and then stopped cold; when they had seen bravery, sadness, courage and strength. They talked of the double wedding and how things had worked out. Once in a while, as they talked, they would get up and take a drink of the cold, clear spring water.